Never Trust a Cricket

Alderbrian Press

Alderbrian Press

Other books by T. D. Sadler and Philip Raymond Sadler:

Wizards War

Books by T. D. Sadler:

The House of Other Worlds

The Reluctant Hero

Wherever the Road Leads

Published by Famulus Press.

Books by Philip Raymond Sadler:

Asblin's Magic Cave

Azophi's Wand

The Sweet Void of Space

The War of the Thirteen Enchantments

The Yarrow Enigma

Wild Wilkenson and The Man in the Moon Prophecy

Suggestions of Stained Glass
Flower Window Art
A coloring book.

Suggestions of Stained Glass
Abstract Art
A coloring book.

Published by Alderbrian Press.

Alderbrian Press

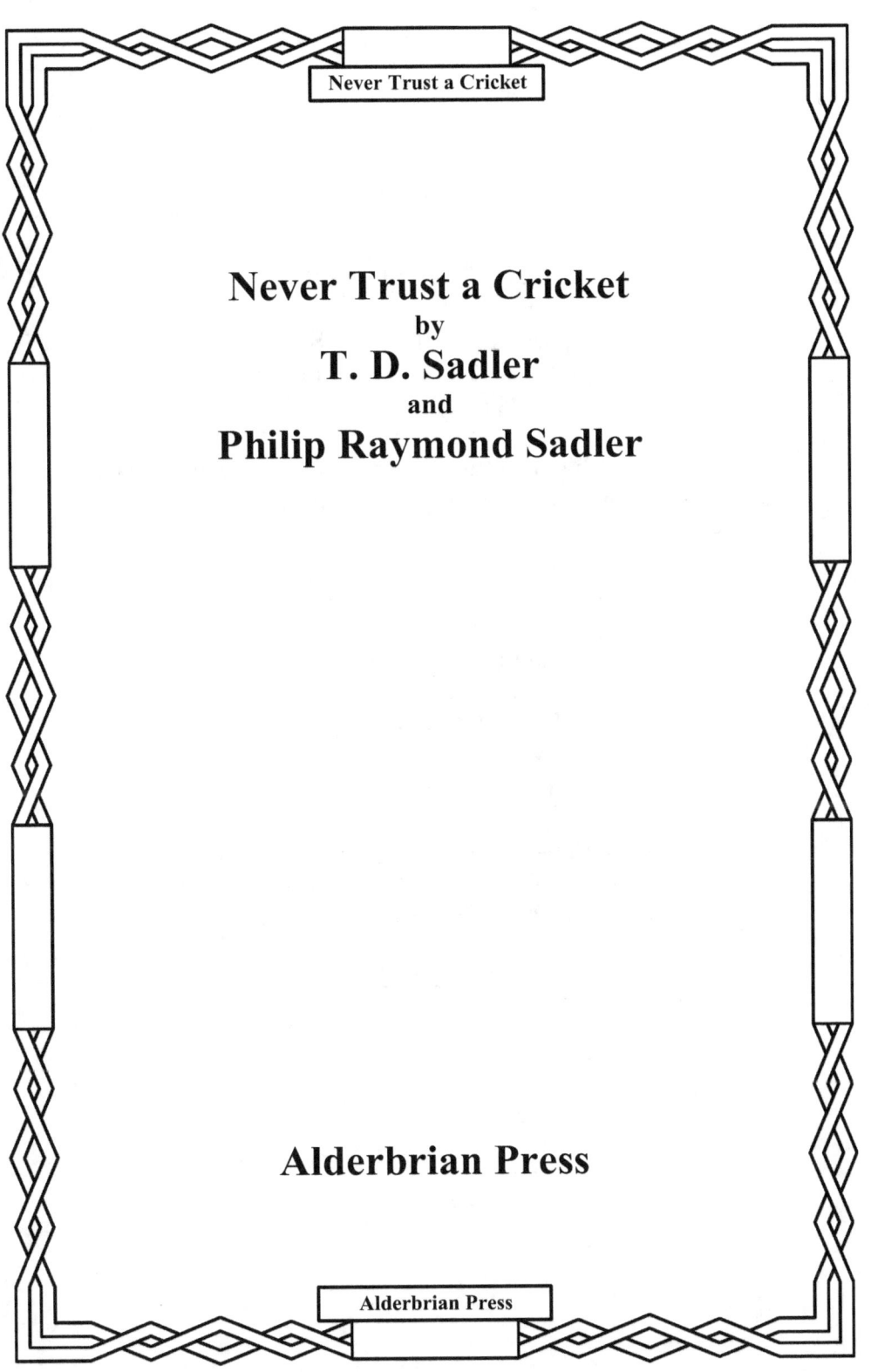

Never Trust a Cricket
by
T. D. Sadler
and
Philip Raymond Sadler

Alderbrian Press

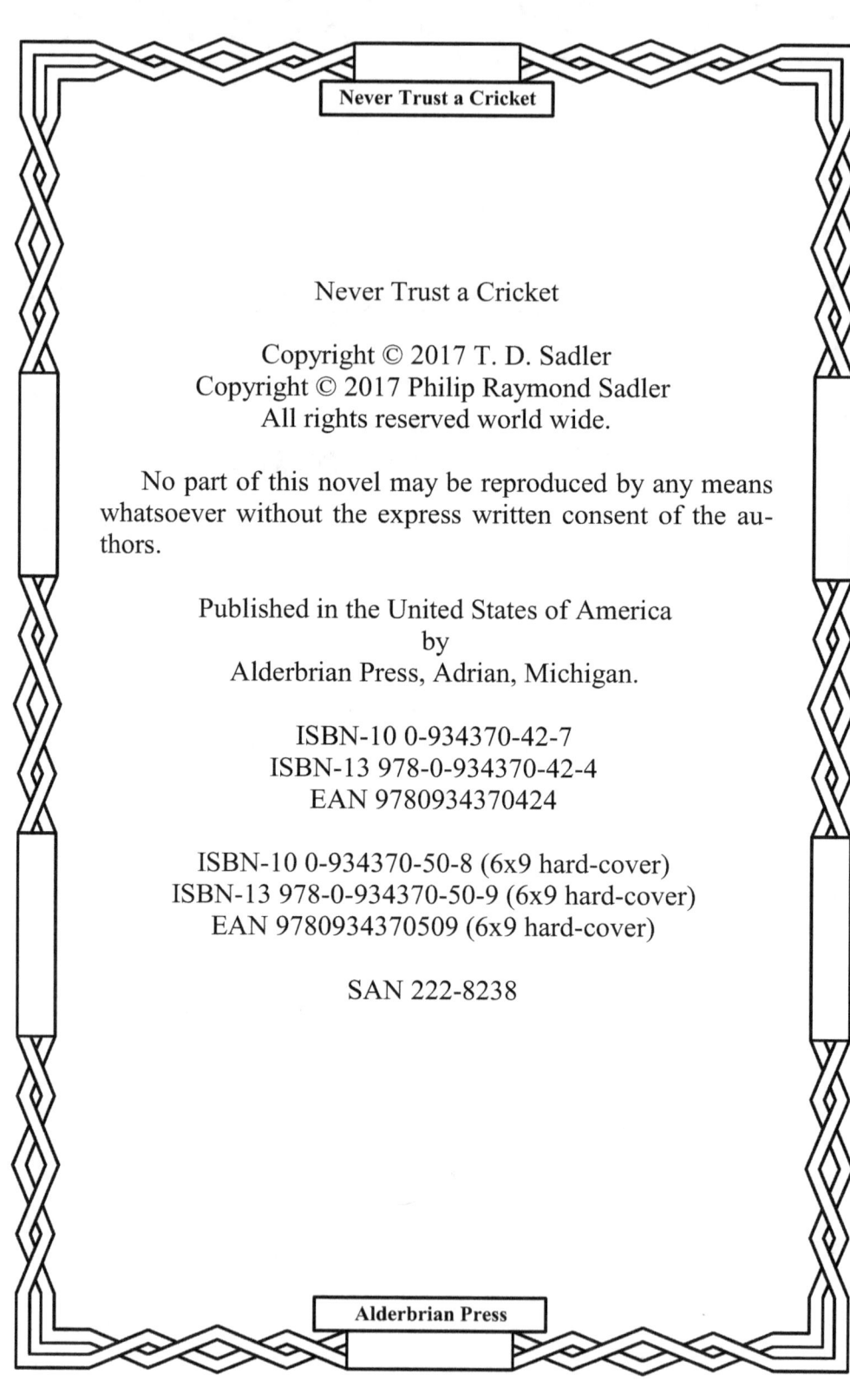

Never Trust a Cricket

Published in the United States of America
by
Alderbrian Press, Adrian, Michigan.

ISBN-10 0-934370-42-7
ISBN-13 978-0-934370-42-4
EAN 9780934370424

ISBN-10 0-934370-50-8 (6x9 hard-cover)
ISBN-13 978-0-934370-50-9 (6x9 hard-cover)
EAN 9780934370509 (6x9 hard-cover)

SAN 222-8238

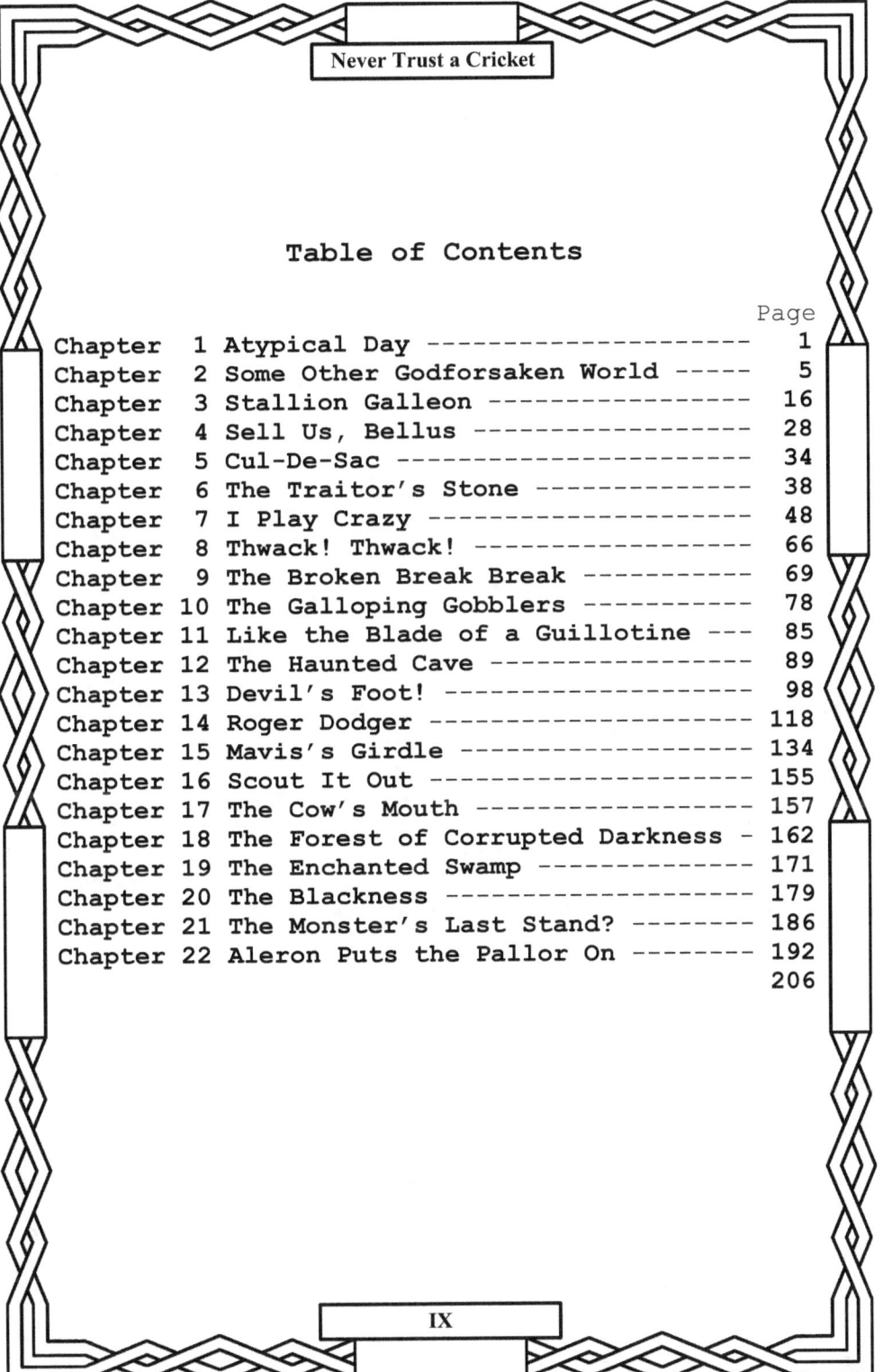

Table of Contents

Chapter 1
Atypical Day

Roger Lincoln stood in front of the full length mirror affixed to the door of his bedroom. He finished buttoning his teddy bear pajama top and ran his brown eyes over his portly form. It was a crummy physique for a twenty-five year old. But it fitted the image of a lazy accountant. Well, not really lazy, just apathetic. He never had inspiration to be otherwise.

He rubbed a pudgy hand through his short, brown hair. His life had always been lousy, and today was no exception. First, as they did at every opportunity, his co-accountants criticized the size of his stomach. Then he spilled coffee on his accounts and spent half the night redoing them. To top it off, on the way home, a man he never met before, picked a fight with him. He used his last five dollars to pay the brute to go away.

A typical day.

The only bright note was the package outside his apartment door. But even this had been marred. When he bent over to pick up the parcel, the seat of his pants ripped open. A burned dinner had not helped his mood.

Now, ready for bed, he felt better and could intelligently consider the contents of the package; a book. He turned out the lights, except for the one on the night stand by the head of the bed and settled down against the pillows to read.

The book had arrived in response to a coupon he clipped from some magazine. The organization which printed it was called the Theocrucians; undoubtedly a nut cult. In fact, the tome had been written by a Southern California quack. Roger did not know this and probably would not have cared.

He flipped the cover, skipped over a warning printed in red, and began reading. The first three pages were filled with pseudo philosophical phrases and unabashed drivel. But the fourth contained the gist of the book.

The proper path to inner harmony and tranquility is so remarkably simple it has been overlooked for thousands of years.

Roger made himself more comfortable.

To attain the state to which he desires, the seeker must fulfill three criteria:

1. He must enjoy a satisfying meal.

2. He should be completely alone.

3. He must be in as perfect a state of silence as possible.

When these objectives have been met, he can pro-

ceed along the path to his ultimate goal.

Roger paused. It occurred to him he had completed those three requirements—mostly. This made him feel strange. With mounting excitement, he read on:

The subject must make himself as comfortable as possible; preferably in a supine position.

Roger smiled; he was lying on his back, his favorite position.

He should close his eyes, take a deep breath, and continuously mentally pronounce his first name backwards.

Roger closed his eyes. But when he drew a deep breath, it turned into a yawn. Disgusted, he tried again. He yawned again. "Nuts," he muttered, "I'm just too sleepy to do it."

He looked at the pocket watch he kept buttoned in his pajama breast pocket. He startled. It was nearly midnight! He tossed the book onto the night stand where it fell open to the warning. When he reached for the lamp switch, he saw the red text again.

"Probably ought to read that before I go further into the book," he mumbled. He snapped the light off and dropped flat of his back. As he drifted off, he wondered what his first name sounded like backwards. Oh, yeah, he thought, Regor. Regor. Regor. Regor. Regor... He started snoring.

Fate, or something else equally twisted, was not kind to him, as usual. The warning read:

Please! Read this Introduction!

*There **is** a danger in this book! Many of my students have attempted the exercises herein while they were either **tired** or **depressed**. As a result, they have been whisked into one of many Alternate Earths! These Earths are hodgepodges of aspects of our Earth, mixed with natural aspects of those Alternate Earths. I know of no one who has ever **returned** from **any** of those Alternate Earths!*

*It is thereby strongly **suggested** and **advised** that you practice my exercises **upon rising**. This is when there is the **least chance** of your being **lulled to sleep** and **lost**!*

*Remember! **This is for your own protection!** Abide by it and, as I have promised on the slick back cover, you **shall** gain a more meaningful, enjoyable and rewarding life through my Self-Improvement Plan!*

Roger turned onto his side. Regor, he dreamed, in huge black letters against a long white cloud. Regor. Regor. Regor.

There was a tremendous flash of lightning and a horrendous thunderclap outside his bedroom window, followed by a terrifying sensation of falling and a painful jolt of landing.

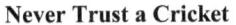
Chapter 2

Some Other Godforsaken World

Roger was so startled he gaped at what he saw. He rubbed his eyes. He even prayed. But it appeared true nonetheless! He was inside a huge dead tree! It was lighted by oil lamps on shelves against the walls.

There were three purple benches arranged in a semicircle. They were covered by hundreds of bottles and vases, and a few tubes filled with liquids bubbling above Fisher burners.

Two strange men were between him and the benches. Their backs were half to him and they were kneeling on the floor in front of a porcelain bedpan from which a thick blue smoke was curling.

Roger dazedly examined the men.

One was over six feet tall. He had curly red hair that parted in the middle. His unfortunate face was leathery, with a long, thin nose. His mustache dangled to his shoulders, his beard trailed behind him; forked at the tip. He was wearing a soiled blue robe and black boots.

The other man was about three feet high. His hair

was short and brown. He was dressed in a short sleeved shirt and a pair of corduroy slacks, both of an ugly green hue. His boots were black. His arms showed that he was tanned. Roger could not see his face.

The robed man reached up, took a bottle off one of the benches and dropped it into the bedpan. When nothing happened to the blue smoke he stood up and kicked the bedpan upside down, splashing a chartreuse liquid over one wall of the tree. The bottle had apparently been dissolved by the goop, for there was no broken glass anywhere.

Roger shakily picked himself up off a pile of mosquito netting. When he started forward, he tripped over a large beaker and landed on his hip on the floor.

The short man scrambled off his knees and both men spun around in surprise.

"You ain't *underwear!*" the robed man shouted.

"I—I'm Roger Lincoln," Roger said. His head was spinning. "And I think something ugly has transpired."

"This ain't no time to venture into the tragedy of your birth," the robed man said. "How'd you *gleeb* in here?"

"I—I don't know," Roger said. "I was asleep, in bed, at home and—Wham! I was here, sore and scared!"

"You didn't use the door?" the dwarf quavered.

Roger thought the dwarf resembled a miniature

version of all the insult comics he hated, but he did not seem as nasty as they acted on stage. "No," he said. "I fell outta—" He peered at the blackened ceiling. "Outta nowhere and my bedroom, I guess."

The robed man slapped himself on the back of his neck with both hands. "*Finzezo!*" he said. "I conjure for *underwear*, and I get a *fat boy!*"

"You *what*?" Roger said.

"What country you hike from?" the robed man asked.

"The United States of America."

"Backwoods, huh?" the robed man mused. "Well, no matter. If it's on the world, I'll probably be able to send you back there. I hope desperately."

"What country is this?" Roger asked. His head was still spinning. He knew this event was too real to be a dream. And he could not understand why they had not heard of the United States before.

"Snooglela," the dwarf said proudly.

Roger coughed. "Snoogle—what?" he said.

"Snooglela," the dwarf said.

"What *world*?" Roger asked, feeling more unsteady.

"*The* world, *teapot*," the dwarf said. "*HackHell*. Is there any *other* with semi-intelligent, pseudo life?"

"Yes!" Roger shouted. He shook his head to stop the spinning but it only became worse. "Earth! Terra! My world!"

"*Earth?*" the robed man said.

"*Terra!*" the dwarf whispered.

"*My* world!" Roger shouted. He sat down hard on the mosquito netting. "Where *my* country, *my* apartment, and *my* bed are!"

The dwarf's eyebrows rose. "Alvisor!" he nearly shrieked. "It's from some *other* godforsaken world!"

Alvisor swallowed so hard and repeatedly it sounded like cows munching corn. He took a deep breath. "All the way from some *other* planet!" he marveled. "Right to *my* lab! *Good Glod*! What *power*!—How'd I do it?" He grabbed Roger by the lapels of his pajamas and demanded: "*How'd I do it?*"

Roger turned white. He whistled seven choruses of the Major-Domo Marching Song. "I don't know," he was finally able to croak. "I'm the *victim*, not the *criminal*!"

"I guess I *could* repeat the spell I was performing before you appeared," Alvisor said. "If another you comes, *Wham!* I've got it again! *Power!*" He released Roger's lapels and executed a short dance of elation.

"Do whatever you want," Roger said. His head was spinning less. "But *send* me back home! It's your obligation. I didn't *ask* to come here. You *ripped* me out of the warmth of my bed, like some hulking monster. You've *got* to send me back!"

Alvisor wiped a tear from his cheek, using a tip of his beard. "Wasn't trying to be no monster," he said. "Was trying to make some underwear. Cold here at night, sometimes. Me and Wilkin wanted to be warm. That's all. Didn't *mean* to bring you here."

"All right," Roger said. His head was settled now, in spite of the eerie impact of his being on another world. "I'm sorry. I didn't have the right to yell at you. But you see how it is, don't you? I'm an alien. I wouldn't fit in on your world. I'd guess. Would I?"

The dwarf shrugged. He pulled a wrinkled paper pack from a pocket of his slacks and lit a cigarette with one of the Fisher burners.

"Probably not," Roger said, when the others did not speak. "So you've a duty to send me back to Earth; my world."

"I'll try," Alvisor said with uncertainty. He used the toe of his left boot to tip the bedpan onto its bottom. He took a vial off one of the benches and poured a brown liquid into the pan. He added black powder from a flask and the mixture began issuing gray smoke. He threw several dozen chemicals into a beaker, swished them about and drank the resulting purple mixture. He tossed more chemicals into another beaker, added others, and still others. He drank this. His hair stood on end, he turned around and shouted: "Psychic powers, don't take hours! Coalesce fast for this spell I cast!"

A shiny black Mess formed and floated in the mixture in the bedpan. It blinked one of its many orange eyes and spat at Roger from one of its multiple mouths.

Alvisor shouted a second verse: "Lift the boy when I say! Take him home; make him stay!"

A green glow enveloped the Mess and the bedpan began to gyrate.

Alvisor twisted his beard tips around his neck and shouted a final verse: "Psychic might! All is tight! Ply the Light! Set things right!"

The Mess crackled. It and the green glow vanished with a popping sound, leaving the bedpan motionless on the floor. The mixture and the smoke turned blue.

Alvisor dropped a square bottle into the bedpan. The mixture turned chartreuse but the smoke remained blue. He and Wilkin looked over their shoulders hopefully.

Roger glared back. "I didn't *return!*" he shouted. "Do you hear me? You *hairy, nondescript, mother!*"

Alvisor kicked the bedpan upside down, splashing the chartreuse liquid where the first batch had gone. He sat down on one of the benches. "I don't understand it," he said. "I did it *all* the same as before, except I used the return form of the verses." He shrugged. "Frankly—if you want frankness—if you can stand the truth." He daubed his red beard at his eyes. "I'm a near fake; a minor trick player, due to age. I've lost most of my memory of spells and most of my magic powers. There must have been an outside influence involved. If I don't know what it was, I can't re-create it to complete the conjure."

Roger bit the knuckles of his hands for a moment, like a fat squirrel eating corn on the cob. "I'm stuck here forever!" he shouted. "Is *that* what you are saying?" He plopped flat on his back on the mosquito netting and mournfully eyed his round stomach.

"That outside influence," Alvisor said. "What was it? What's the last thing you remember before you butted in here?"

"I was dreaming," Roger said. "There was this long, bright white cloud with a huge black word repeated along it. I was reading the word over and over. Then there was real lightning and thunder outside my window and I was here."

"What word?" Alvisor said. He was keenly apprehensive.

"My first name backwards," Roger said. "Regor."

Alvisor hopped off the bench and slapped a hand over Roger's mouth. "Never speak *that* Word!" he ordered. "It's *the* Power Word! Only *one* man on Hack-Hell can handle *that* Word!" He helped Roger to stand up. "You've supplied the outside influence that got you here and messed up my perfect spell. We had one hell of a shot of lightning outside my tree from a passing thunderstorm, just before you wafted in. So, that Power Word you were dreaming caused synchronization of the vibratory energy of the two lightnings, and created a space warp you fell through when your lightning knocked you out of your bed."

"Come to think of it, I did fall out of the sack about then," Roger realized, "and landed on your floor instead of my slippers. Does all this mean you can get me home now?"

"No," Alvisor said. "*I* can't send you to your world, but I know one really good magician who *can*. There are only two—maybe—truly mighty magicians left on the world. I know the most powerful one actually exists and he can even create space warps. He'll get you home. I swear it!" He chuckled happily. "That Power Word you said helped me to remember all that warp stuff and who discovered and proved it."

Roger dried his eyes, with his thumbs. "Is Alvisor telling the truth, Wilkin?" he said.

"Yeah," Wilkin said. "I've heard of this same Magus before. He's real spooky; makes soap out of rocks and turns spoons into nightmares. If anybody would know where he is, Al would. He's a regular walking, talking, geographical en—encyclopediable." He wrinkled his nose and looked foolish, but endearing, for a dirty little man.

Roger and Alvisor laughed.

"He's the only magician who can muster the power for warps, and he won't share the arcane secrets with anybody. The chances of simultaneous lightning on our earth and yours occurring again in your lifetime, Roger," Alvisor said, "are almost not possible at the moment you think the Power Word. So I'll just have to take you to the right man."

"When can we start?" Roger said eagerly.

"Now, if you want," Alvisor said. "The guy we're going to see, picked a home place, for energy reasons, that's high up and hard to reach. There's a couple of nasty areas we have to pass through to get there. And we'll have to travel a hundred miles or so."

"That shouldn't be a problem," Roger said. "I'm game."

"Me too!" Wilkin said.

"Go out back and lock up the old equipment shed, then, Wilkin, while I explain the route to Roger," Alvisor said. He took a key from a pocket of his robe and held it out.

"Right!" Wilkin said. He grabbed the key and scampered out the door of the tree.

"My path leads to a road," Alvisor said. "We'll follow that into Brown Willow and buy a wagon and supplies for the trip. We'll go across the small zone where the Franchised Bandits roam. Then through the Wilderness to a Frontier Town. From there, we'll take a step or two across the WharlWash Desert and navigate a mountain pass called The Cow's Mouth. There upon we'll hit The Enchanted Swamp. Then we'll knock on Aleron's—the big magician's—front door. It would be impolite, though safer, to go to his back door." He smiled charmingly, for a big dirty man. "Nothing to get excited about. Yet."

Roger smiled in naive admiration. "Hey," he said. "Do you have some shoes I can borrow?" He knew his teddy bear pajamas could stand the trip, but his feet could not, if he should have to walk much.

Alvisor stepped behind the middle bench and handed over a pair of dusty clodhoppers.

Roger could not have been more grateful if the shoes had been made of platinum. He slipped them on and laced them tight. He walked into the golden morning sunlight flooding the forest outside the tree. "Are you coming, Alvisor?" he said over his shoulder.

"A minute!" Alvisor said gruffly. "All I ask is a minute! I have to see everything is all right in here."

He turned off the oil lamps and the Fisher burners, bringing pitch darkness. There was a CLOSED sign hanging on a nail in the inside of the door. He turned this around so the letters faced the old wood, took another key from his robe pocket, and locked up the huge tree.

Roger was about to ask why the magician didn't hang the sign on the *outside* of the door, like a normal person, where it could be seen, when he noticed it was somehow showing *through* the wood, with a spooky glow.

They were standing on a well worn dirt path.

Roger could not believe his bedazzled eyes! F-shaped, scarlet leaves grew on the trees, while square, black flowers thrived around the brown trunks.

Wilkin came around the tree and handed the key to the magus. Alvisor dropped it into his pocket, led them along the path, and onto a wide dirt road. There was a forest on each side.

Chapter 3
Stallion Galleon

The fierce black stallions strained at their harnesses as though desperate to escape their confinement. Behind, a great ebony coach rumbled along the dirt road, raising a wide trail of choking dust.

The driver hunched in the hard wooden seat atop the front of the coach. He had the hood of his raven habit pulled down over his bald head. He had been driving all night and his rat-like face showed his fatigue. He could not understand why the Master did not stop, even to rest the horses. They had kept up this galloping longer than he believed any steeds could. But, nothing involving the Master was as he thought it should be; as it would be with any other man.

The road wound between two vast forests, and there seemed to be no end to the lonely territory they crossed. The small towns they raced through were all poverty stricken, or deserted. Why the Master had left his fine castle, was a mystery. But everything the Master did was a bafflement.

As the coach flew around a bend in the road, figures appeared. The driver pulled in the reins, slowing the coach. "Make way for the Master!" he shouted harshly.

Two of the men dove to the left, the third to the right, all rolling into the forests a few feet.

The driver raised his long whip from its receptacle beside him, to inspire the steeds to regain speed.

A voice, deep enough to make a statue's skin crawl, rumbled from the interior of the coach. "Hold, driver! I would visit with these gentlemen!"

The driver stuck the whip into its holder. He hauled in the reins with both hands and kicked the horizontal brake control down with his booted feet, almost standing up with the effort. The great, creaking coach ground slowly to a halt.

The huge stallions, unlike other horses, fidgeted, anxious to continue their galloping, not interested in rest.

"Ask the gentlemen to approach the left window!" the voice commanded.

Roger struggled out of some vines and got to his knees. Asking questions with his expression, he looked at Alvisor.

Wilkin scuttled around the back of the wide coach and huddled with his pals.

"*Don't say anything!*" Alvisor warned Roger. "This guy is *big-stink* important, or he couldn't own that glorified coffin."

"The Master *will* speak with you," the driver announced hoarsely. "You would *favor* yourselves to comply."

Alvisor and Roger helped each other up. Then they helped Wilkin up, realized he was already standing, and put him back on the ground. They edged nervously toward the coach.

The noon sun gleamed off the unmarred black paint like torch light off an obsidian grave stone. The ebony lace curtain on the window rolled up like the eyelid of a squatting lizard. A massive, shadowy shape, with gleaming eyes, glared at the trio. "Where are you bound?" the basso profundo voice demanded.

"Brown Willow," Alvisor said. He was reluctantly leaning closer to see the figure better.

"Why?"

"To buy a wagon for a trip," Alvisor said.

"Your names?"

"Roger, Wilkin, and Alvisor, the Magician," Alvisor said.

"Magician?"

The deep interest in the voice made Alvisor queasy and uneasy. "Yes," he said hesitantly.

"You *will* ride with me," the shape said. "I shall pass through Brown Willow."

Roger shook his head so many times and so quickly, his poor eyes rattled. "I'd rather walk, *sir*," he croaked. "I'm fat. I need the exercise. Lots of it."

"*You will ride with me!*" the figure commanded. The door flew open, with no movement from the occupant, and a set of black steps unfolded toward the road. "*Hurry!* You are squandering *my* priceless time!"

Alvisor grabbed Roger. "Listen, don't you say another word the whole trip! I'll do all the talking. You keep shut too, Wilkin. This guy could kill us on the spot, and no one would complain. If we refuse to ride now, he just might. *You understand?*"

Roger nodded his head.

Wilkin gnawed on one of his thumbs, and one of Roger's thumbs, and one of Alvisor's thumbs.

Alvisor forced himself to climb into the dark, musty coach. Roger and Wilkin came in as one man. Wilkin was hanging from the back of Roger's P. J. top. When they were seated across from the figure, the steps folded up and the door snapped shut.

The driver plied his whip to the air above the nervous horses and they responded like a bullet fired from an enormous gun, seeming to achieve a flat gallop instantly.

The lace curtain lowered and the darkness was almost total inside the soundless coach.

Alvisor iron-gripped Roger's wrist. Roger squeezed Wilkin's neck. Wilkin was now cowering on Roger's lap.

Roger noted the coach did not bounce, though it should have been doing the Charleston at its current speed.

"You claim you are a magician," the bottomless voice said. "What degree?"

"I used to be triple A," Alvisor said. "But I'm sliding rapidly."

"You can still conjure?"

"Will it make any difference, sir?" Wilkin peeped fearfully. His imagination was working overtime, hallucinating ball bombs, knives and small cannons on the seat next to the imposing shape.

"You can conjure?" the man insisted.

"Sometimes," Alvisor said. "But I usually blow the job. I just get by on Low Conjures. Nothing *you* could use. *I'm sorry.*"

"What is the purpose of your companions?"

"Just pals," Alvisor said hastily. "We're on vacation."

"Vacation implies work," the man rumbled. "What labor does the dwarf perform?"

"My assistant," Alvisor said.

"And the boy?"

"He's next to worthless," Alvisor said, straining his sad, whimpering intellect, "he's a poet."

"This explains his strange clothing," the man observed. The tone of his voice shouted suspicion and interest. More interest than was reasonable.

"May—may I ask *your* occupation, *sir*?" Alvisor said.

"No."

"Your name, *sir*?"

"No."

"*Thank you, sir*," Alvisor said fervently.

The figure's featureless, but threatening head, turned to Roger. "*You* will reply to my questions, please. Your full name?"

Roger squeezed Alvisor's leg.

Alvisor only trembled.

"Roger Lincoln," Roger squeaked.

"Your home?"

"I—I live with Alvisor, sir."

"Your birth place?"

"Wi—Wilkin's home."

"Where is that?" the voice said, with impatience.

"Green Wood Village," Wilkin said quickly.

"You lie, Roger Lincoln," the figure accused. "You have an accent not from this area, or from any other region I know. You have softer features than these rustics, and even most of my contemporaries. Now! The *truth*, Lincoln!"

The coach abruptly began slowing. The trio lurched toward the other seat, almost falling into the man's lap. He was unaffected by the deceleration, and all they could tell about him was, he wore a habit, gloves and boots; all black.

"Brown Willow, Master!" the driver shouted.

There was a long electric pause.

Alvisor's breathing could be heard echoing throughout the coach.

Wilkin began biting his fingernails like an air hammer chops cement.

Roger's heart had not beaten in two minutes.

"Very well," the figure rumbled. "*We shall meet again*! My questions *shall* be answered *then*. Go!"

The door flew open, spearing the interior of the coach with sunlight, none of which fell on the Master, almost as if it were afraid to.

Alvisor, Roger and Wilkin threw themselves out before the steps had fully unfolded. They tumbled into an undignified heap on the road, beside a prehistoric shack some yards from Brown Willow.

The driver cracked the whip like a cannon shot and the stallions sailed away, leaving the trio in a cloud of stinking dust thrown up by the grooved hooves of the horses and the studded wheels of the coach.

An elderly man wobbled out of the shack and stood staring at the trio. His long white hair and incredible beard were matted together, so he looked more like a senior lion, than a human being. His thick hair and whiskers appeared to double as his clothes.

Alvisor rolled Roger off Wilkin and helped them stand up. "What the hell you staring at?" he snapped.

The ancient boomer cackled with offensive joy. "*Dead men*," he said. "I always stare at them *dead men*!"

"We aren't perished *yet*?" Wilkin said offendedly.

"Yes you are. When you ride with, *such as that*, in

that carrion carriage, you're dead. It ain't caught up with you yet, but it will. *Such as that*, kills by proximity. If I hadn't been in my hut when, *such as that*, paused here, I'd be a dead one, too."

"Who was, *such as that*?" Roger asked.

"You don't know?" the old man squealed. He looked like he was going to quit life on the spot. He rolled his bloodshot eyes toward the heavens. "He don't know *The Monster*, and he was *riding* with it!" he shouted with astonishment.

"*The Monster*!" Alvisor screamed. "You sure positive?"

The homely old man grinned toothlessly. "Been sure of that one since I was but ten," he said. "Be sure of him longer than you'll live, too."

"You've heard of The Monster before?" Roger said. "Why's he called The Monster? Will we really die? Why did you make us go into the coach if you knew about him? I'll kill myself now and save The Monster the effort. Maybe he'll spare me, then."

"You could slay yourself to please him and he'd slaughter you twice more anyway," the old man said. "Can I have your valuables? They won't help you in the earth. I can get a new comb, or some bean leaves to gum on."

"If you don't get the hell away from here," Alvisor shouted, "you'll be gumming my boot!"

The wizened citizen stuck up his fingers in obscene

gestures. "Feller tries to help and only gets meaned on. Serves you right to croak. Hope he gets you *fast*." He tottered around in a circle and entered his shabby, smelly hovel.

"Who *is* The Monster?" Roger said.

"A legend, I thought," Alvisor said.

"Rather active legend," Roger observed sourly. "Tell me about it."

"Can't," Alvisor said. "I only heard there *was* a legend about The Monster. A very *horrible* man. Never the details."

"Maybe that old fart can enlighten us," Wilkin said.

"If he's correct about us being marked for death, we'd better find out about it," Roger said. "There's no use returning home if I'm doing the croaker shuffle with my ancestors."

"That's probably prattle from a weak mind," Alvisor said. "But, we'll check anyway."

They lined up at the worm holed door of the weathered shack. Alvisor knocked on the portal with Wilkin's forehead.

The old man looked sullen. He started to slam the door in Wilkin's angry face, then he cackled again with offensive joy. "You wanna hear about The Monster, don't you?" he squawked.

"Correct, muscle mind," Alvisor said. He swallowed hard and audibly. It sounded painful. "I'll even *pay* you for your knowledge. *If* you place some *actual* facts predominately in with your *fantasy*."

"*Facts!*" the wrinkled boomer shouted. "They's *all* facts! Nobody could fantasy anything about The *Monster!* Not even this lily white weirdo, in the teddy clothes!"

"Now, see here," Roger said, "anybody who lives with a beard for his pants is a lot—"

"Just talk," Alvisor said, waving Roger to silence.

The cobwebbed senior cackled insultingly and sat down on the dirt, propping himself against the wall of the flimsy hut.

The trio reluctantly stepped closer.

"A sorcerer," mister age squawked. "It's a big, Black Magic Sorcerer. Wants the whole world as its slavery yard. Been after it for sixty years.

"It and Aleron are enemies. It's Only been able to control these four hundred miles around here 'cause Aleron's got the rest.

"Always undoing The Monster's spells and the like. But even Aleron's not strong enough, yet, to destroy The Monster, like he did the last despot Wizard who ran the world into the shit hole and jumped in after.

"Monster's only trouble is, he can't find Aleron to attack. Some of us thinks The Monster can lick old Aleron fierce.

"But nobody knows where Aleron lives. We only feel his magic. He finds out about almost every ugly thing going on. If it's done to somebody innocent, he steps in, in some way, with his misty magic, to help. Though he ain't been doing as much of it lately, for some unknowed reason.

"Since nobody knows where Aleron lives, The Monster speeds around in his casket on wheels, grabbing out of their homes and off the highways and byways, anybody he feels might know.

"If they don't know, or they knows and don't tell him, or he feels they knows and refused to tell, he kills them. You notice, he kills them iffin they didn't know or lied about knowing. Some say he's got hold of The Traitor's Stone and now knows for sure whether you're lying or not."

"You're crazier than a freak working in a hot coal factory," Alvisor said. "Why didn't he kill *us*? We didn't do him any good in his hunt?"

The old man scratched his knee. It, among other things, was projecting out of his snowy beard. "Well, he's getting old now, and Aleron's the only one who knows how to extend youthful life. So that's why The Monster's increasing his pickups lately. He wildly wants that Youth Magic Knowledge. Guess he figured it would waste his time to kill you, or—" He cackled insultingly until his eyes crossed. "Or he's still interested in you and just waiting for a chance to grab you again. Maybe he's checking you out with his slime wallowing spies. He's got thousands of them around

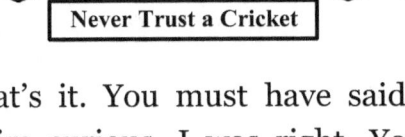
here. Yep, that's it. You must have said something what made him curious. I was right. You *are* dead men. Pay me, before he deads you and *I* get caught in the backlash."

Alvisor placed a coin into the grubby wrinkled palm. "Where does he live, so we can avoid it?" he demanded, holding another coin above the eager hand.

"Like with Aleron, nobody knows!" the crinkled boomer said. He snatched the coin with unbelievable speed, leaped to his feet, backed into his shack, and slammed and bolted the door.

Chapter 4

Sell Us, Bellus

BrownWillow was nestled on both sides of the road in a clearing in the forests. It was a medium sized affair, peaceful and charming in the sun.

To Roger, it was very much like an English village of the middle Ages. As he gazed at the weathered mud-and-straw brick buildings quaintly lining the narrow dirt streets, a sensation of warmth rose in him. He felt as though he belonged there. It would be much better to live in BrownWillow than in the bedlam city from which he came.

Alvisor led them through a line of garbage crates to a sleazy looking wagon shop just off the main street. It was a two story, clapboard building, with huge picture windows. "There are a couple of other places in town," he said, "but this guy ain't so mercenary. Besides, I know him and he'll probably dish me out a great discount."

They passed through the very wide, open door and paused. Two partially finished, shabby wagons sat in the center of the main room. Several others were being started nearby. The workmen resembled warm things without brains or human qualities, dressed in dirty togas. One or two wiped at drool. They all ignored the trio.

Alvisor spied the owner coming out of a back room. "Come on," he said, "I'll introduce you."

They barely made it through the obstacle course of wagon parts and dullard workmen alive.

"Bellus, old friend, I'd like you to meet a couple of other pals of mine. This is Roger," Alvisor said, pulling Roger from behind him. "Leggo the robe!" he scolded.

Bellus paced forward. He was seven feet tall and there were more lines on his wide, weather-browned face than on a troupe of old crones. He held out a massive mitt. "Pleased ta beat—I mean, meet'cha," he boomed. "Ya knowed Al a long spell?"

This walking mass of muscle and scar tissue reminded Roger of the man who picked a fight with him on Earth. He automatically reached for a five dollar bill. He was jolted to reality when he did not find a pocket on his pajama seat. He overcame his fright and shook his head.

"Dat's okay," Bellus said. "Ya gotta watch him clost. He's downright sneaky and dishonest when he gets the chancet. So don't let him."

Roger shook hands and leaped back to a safer distance.

"And this," Alvisor said, "is Wilkin."

Wilkin stepped forward. With a timid smile, he stuck his hand out for Bellus to shake. Not actually wanting him to. "Hi," he said, craning his neck painfully.

"Hi ya, half legs," Bellus blustered. "Ya look like ya was picked before ya had a chancet ta get ripe. Har! Har! But, any friend of Al's is a friend of mine?" He turned to Alvisor. "Now, what kin I do ya fer—er—fer ya?"

"It's like this, Bellus," Alvisor said. "We're going on a long trip and we need transportation. Just something that will get us there and back."

"How much?" Bellus demanded.

Alvisor feigned amazement reasonably well. "Huh?" he said.

"How much do ya wanna pay fer da wagging?" Bellus said.

"Well," Alvisor said, actually taken aback, "I thought we might look them over before we decide."

"We kin gape at anything ya wants all the day long and into the weary, dragging night," Bellus grumbled, "but when ya gets ready ta buy a wagging, ya'll wind up taking the cheapest one in da jernt. So, how much glod do ya actual wanna *pay*?"

Alvisor's shrewd eyes rotated clockwise once. "What do you offer for five glod?" he said.

"*Five* swaks of glod!" Bellus shouted. "Da damn wheels cost more'en *five* swaks of glod!"

"How about six glod?" Alvisor conceded.

"*Six* glod!" Bellus yelled louder. "Do ya see dat ijit sitting in da corner? I pays *him* more'en *six* glod a week just fer putting da cotter pins inta da axles ta keep da damn wheels from falling off!"

"Do you have anything for seven glod, then?" Alvisor demanded.

"I always knowed ya was a *cheap teeth*!" Bellus roared. "But I didn't think ya was *dat* cheap! *Seven glod my tits*!"

"All right, *thief*!" Alvisor shouted. "I'll give you *ten* glod for a wagon! And that's *nine* times what the damn *wrecks* are *worth*! Now, show it to us!"

Bellus led them to the rear room. He indignantly threw the door open and stood aside.

The trio stared at a four wheeled platform; a wagon without side one. Its only major feature was a backless bench bolted to the bed.

"*Dat's* what ya *gets* fer *ten* glod," Bellus huffed.

Alvisor considered the conveyance curiously. "Is it a *good* wagon?" he said insultingly.

The wagon maker struck a proud pose and appeared self-righteous. "I stands behind each and ever wagging I craft and fence—er—sell!" he proclaimed.

Wilkin snickered. "That way, his dumb customers can't run over him when they leave in an insulted rage," he said. "I don't think that thing can go backwards."

"Or so he can be certain to shove them out the door before they fall apart," Roger said.

"Where'd ya get dim inept jesters?" Bellus said. "At a rummage sale run by aged lunatics? If so, ya got ya-self screwed!"

"Rudely ignore them," Alvisor said. He made an enviably ugly face at his companions.

They were impressed.

"I'm glad I ain't da one has ta put up with dere rip-a-part-tee. I'd bump dere gourds flat," Bellus said. He became smiles. "Since ya and me is such, ugh, good friends, I'll give ya da loan of my mule. *Perviding* ya brings him back with his head, his tail, *and* all four of his legs."

"Dead or alive?" Alvisor said.

"Alive, if ya kin make it," Bellus said. "Otherwise, I'll just have ta charge ya nine glod fer da wear and tear ta da mule."

"I could *buy* a damned mule for nine glod!" Alvisor charged.

"Dat's just what ya'll be doing if ya brings him back very deceased," Bellus said.

"*Robber baron fiend*," Alvisor said, sounding like he was complimenting the merchant. "It's a deal!"

"Okay dokey," Bellus said. He accepted the shiny glod, counting un-trustingly along with insulted Alvisor. "Ya kin take da wagging out dese rear doors. Da mule is out back in da stable. Try not ta bother da wife when ya fetches him!"

"Here, Wilkin," Alvisor said. "Go purchase some food and water-filled bags while we're fighting this wagon." He handed Wilkin some glod and the dwarf slipped out the rear portal.

*** * ***

When Roger and Alvisor left the stable, they were limping and pulling straw out of their ears and noses. Apparently, the mule had buried itself up to its ears in straw and they were forced to dig the sad old animal out before they could hitch it to the wagon.

The mule looked mummified and walked like there were no joints in its legs. It also seemed indifferent to its situation. But, so does a corpse.

"For a while there," Alvisor said, "I couldn't tell which was the mule and which was the missus."

Roger sniggered shamefully.

They climbed aboard the wagon and Alvisor directed the animal to the nearest supply store on the main street. It was a squatty building with grease paper windows. BUY SHOP was carved crummily above the mud portal.

Wilkin was asleep atop a pile of goods on the boardwalk.

Alvisor climbed from the wagon, with outstanding ineptness, and twisted the dwarf's nose.

"I bought 'em fair and four posted!" Wilkin shouted. He saw it was only Alvisor, and wiped his brow. Then he wiped his own brow.

Under Alvisor's stern and astute supervision, Roger and Wilkin reloaded the wagon.

It took less than two hours.

In another ten minutes of being seated, they were off across charming BrownWillow, toward the rear gates.

Chapter 5
Cul-de-sac

The mega-coach was parked on a side street in BrownWillow near the rear gates.

The Monster's voice sounded telepathically just beside the driver's ear. "Yes, master?" he said, knowing his words would be magically detected by The Monster.

"Would you vacation in this territory?"

"I don't know, master."

"What unusual sights are here for them to view? What fine cultural attractions or collectible goods upon which to spend their hard earned glod?"

The driver smiled wickedly, but did not voice his lurid thoughts. "Nothing, master," he said. "Nothing those—*gentlemen*—would wish to see."

"So, as I thought, they are *not* vacationing."

"Then, why are they here, master? It can't be just stupidity."

"Why am *I* here?"

The driver shivered though the sun was baking his habit uncomfortably hot. "You have not said, but I have thought it is to destroy vile Aleron. *Forgive me for thinking, master!*"

"You seldom do so well," The Monster said. "And, this time, you are correct. I seek Aleron. They must also be seeking him. I have information he is somewhere in this area. They are coming this way. One of them must know where Aleron resides."

"Shall we waylay them, Master? There is a nice cul-de-sac around the corner. The abandoned houses forming it will give us privacy. All we need do is trick them into our snare."

There was a long silence.

The driver knew better than to disturb the master unless his words were laden with information.

"Which one knows?" The Monster finally said beside the driver's ear.

"You wish me to think *again*, master?" He sounded insulted as well as frightened.

"You have done well, once, try again," The Monster said sardonically.

"The dwarf is all mouth, master. The boy is—strange. But the old magician? He knows much. So much, he has forgotten he knows it."

"Have you been practicing thinking?" The Monster demanded.

The driver turned a laudable shade of white. "Yes, master! Forgive me, master! *Please!*"

"You require more practice. But you have improved.

Yes, the old toad of a magician knows where Aleron is. And the boy *is* uncanny. Almost as if he is not of *this* world."

This time there was an even longer silence.

The sun grew hotter on the driver's hunched and perspiring back.

"Not of *this* world," The Monster said telepathically.

"A ghost, master?"

"Did I ask you to think again?"

"Forgive me, master! I will beat myself tonight!"

"It can only be a *Genie*. Yes, there is nothing within my magic tomes to explain such fair features, except the Lore of The Genies." He mumbled angrily for several moments. "My father vowed he slew the final Genie one hundred years ago! But, he foully lied to me constantly. He feared me. Feared my power, and my instinctual knowledge of the arcane. There still *are* Genies, and this Roger Lincoln *is* one of them!"

"A Genie, master!" the driver shouted. He was even more terrified of Genies than he was of The Monster. "But a *Genie* is *all* magic! If a fat Genie is going to Aleron! *Master—*"

"Yes! Yes! Aleron can easily control a Genie! I will be destroyed seconds after the Genie meets Aleron! *I* must control the Genie!"

"What about the Genie's *magic*, master?"

"It will be mostly blocked as Aleron's magic has been dampened by my Obstruction Spell!"

"What if you cannot control the Genie, master?"

"If not, after they have answered my polite inquiries, they will all die! Now, stop thinking until I command it! But keep practicing. In about twenty years, your mind might be useful to me! Or for nose picking."

"Yes, master! Forgive me, master! I'll try, master!"

"They approach!" The Monster telepathed with excitement. "Now, cut them off! Force them into the cul-de-sac, or fry!"

Chapter 6

The Traitor's Stone

"Look out!" Roger shouted.

Alvisor jerked the reins to the right, veering the wagon.

The great coach turned at them.

Alvisor sighted the cul-de-sac, unaware it was a dead-end, and reined the old mule stiff leggedly into it.

The creaking coach followed.

"We're trapped!" Wilkin warned. "These houses are all boarded up! There's no way between them!"

Alvisor reined the mule to a full turn, to slip the wagon between the coach and one of the houses at the mouth of the cul-de-sac, but the turn was too sharp. The wagon flipped onto its side, spilling cargo and trio onto the sand of the vacant lot.

The coach ground to a halt. The doors swept open and their steps unfolded. The driver scrambled down and stood at the right hand door.

As The Monster descended the steps, the coach almost tipped over with his weight. He was still concealed by his ebony habit. He whispered and the great horses ceased fidgeting as if hypnotized.

Roger rolled off Wilkin and Alvisor and jumped to his feet. He grabbed Wilkin up and started running beside Alvisor, around the left side of the coach, toward the mouth of the cul-de-sac.

"Joints of knees, now you freeze!" The Monster intoned. "Feet approach this waiting coach!" His power was like bands of iron on their knees and legs.

Roger resisted as hard as he could, straining until he felt his heart pounding angrily in his chest and causing a painful throbbing in his head, but his legs turned him around and carried him swiftly toward the glistening coach.

Alvisor moved precisely beside Roger, same speed, same length of pace, until they were halted within three feet of The Monster. The darkness within his hood prevented them from seeing his face.

Roger did not even try. He kept mentally commanding his legs to take him backwards at light speed. They continued to betray him, rooting him to the spot.

Wilkin hung in Roger's arms like a pugnacious doll stuffed with wet sand. The dwarf's mouth yawned open and his drool was forming an odious pool at Roger's feet.

"Shall I hurt them, master?" the driver begged. His rat-like face showed he was overjoyed at the prospect. He slipped a knife out of a sheath inside his habit.

"Take the dwarf first," The Monster ordered. "Place him on the sand on his back. We shall try the stone on him. I doubt he has brains enough to know which part of his body his filthy ass is on, but I have had greater surprises in life. He *might* possess some knowledge I can use."

Roger held onto Wilkin with all his strength.

The driver wrestled the dwarf away and threw him, face up, onto the sand.

Roger tried to speak but was totally paralyzed now. Alvisor was wagging his tongue between his teeth but, otherwise, was just as useless.

Wilkin lay drooling. He had his eyes squeezed shut. He did not want to see what was preparing to abuse him. Or how it was about to do so.

"When can *I* hurt them, master?" the driver begged, hopping up an down like an excited puppy. He was sharpening the knife on the top of his bald, scaly head.

"You act like a dog!" The Monster said. "Sit! Be *silent*! Mutt!"

The driver dropped in his tracks, shaking with fear. But he held his precious knife under his arm in case the master changed his nefarious mind.

The Monster reached into a pocket of his habit and withdrew a small, black-leather pouch. He opened this and took out a red gem.

Alvisor recognized the mystic ruby. He began sweating and searching his dried up brain for spells and psychic energy. He was sure he had set some back, at least a hundred times, during his squandered youth. Just for such ugly, unwanted, unwarranted, joyless occasions. He had succeeded in recalling this fact, maybe he could remember the phrase to release the energy. *He had better*!

The Monster bent close to Wilkin and placed the gem on the dwarf's slack forehead. The jewel slid onto the sand twice before The Monster realized why. He grabbed the driver by the habit front and wiped Wilkin's sweaty forehead dry. This time, the accursed gem stayed where it was placed.

The Monster let the driver go and stood towering over Wilkin like a cliff over a pebble. "You *will* speak!" he commanded. "You *will* answer my clever and insightful questions! Tell me all you know of Aleron!"

Wilkin's tongue stood straight up and wagged. His face twisted and he looked like a cowboy who missed taking the bull by the horns. "He turns rocks into soap, and spoons into nightmares!" he said. "If anybody would know where he lives, old Al would. He's a regular walking geographical en—encyclopediable!"

The Monster turned massively to Alvisor. "So, you *are* the knowledgeable bone head!" He took the gem off Wilkin's forehead. "Place this tall, red, noxious weed on the sand, driver!"

The driver dropped his knife and threw himself at Alvisor's ankles, knocking the magician face down on

the driver's back. The driver rolled them both over, scrambled to his feet and retrieved his knife.

Alvisor's beard was curled up, covering his face.

"Move his damned beard aside!" The Monster ordered.

When the driver reached out, the beard lashed him on the hand with its forked tips and re-coiled over the magician's face. The driver growled with pain and anger. He dropped his knife and made a two handed grab. The beard stung him on both hands before it re-coiled.

"If he will not move it himself, cut it off!" The Monster shouted.

Alvisor's beard went limp and slid off his face, into a fuzzy heap by his head.

The Monster placed the gem on Alvisor's forehead and leaned close.

Alvisor could see only darkness and gleaming eyes inside the hood. He attempted to swallow his tongue, to keep from talking. Then he continued ransacking his brain for energy reserves.

"Where does Aleron live!" The Monster demanded.

"Pardon?" Alvisor said, with a gasp.

"I will *not* repeat the question!"

"You want the short route, the long route, or the beside the way, rosy, scenic route?"

"Speak or die!" The Monster roared.

The driver snatched his knife off the sand and pressed its blade to Alvisor's throat.

Alvisor snaked his beard around the driver, pinning the man's arms to his sides. He began slamming the driver side to side against the sand, causing the man to grunt with each impact.

"Stop!" The Monster shouted. "Stop! Stop! Stop!" He jumped up and down in his tracks uncontrollably for a moment, crunching the sand under his black boots with his unnatural weight.

Alvisor laughed. He had found some of his hidden magic energy. He threw the fuming driver atop the coach, then whipped his beard at The Monster's head.

There was a blinding flash of crimson light. The beard became as stiff as rock. The Monster took off a glove. He stuck out a stubby white forefinger and scarlet fire jetted forth. He held the flaming digit to the tips of Alvisor's beard. The animated whiskers became soft at Alvisor's urging but remained in mid air, through The Monster's power. The Monster blew out his finger and pulled his ebony glove on.

"He lives on Ikkapoor Mountain!" Alvisor said, with a gasp. The insidious gem had finally overcome his energy.

"There is no such mountain!" The Monster roared. His basso profundo voice vibrated the old houses surrounding them. "Your next lie will be your death warrant!"

"It's in The Enchanted Swamp. A large clearing. But, you'll have to go through The Cow's Mouth, to get there!"

"Master!" the driver shouted, in horror. He was standing monkey-like, knife in hand, atop the glistening coach. "The Cow's Mouth!"

"Get down here and prepare to depart!" The Monster ordered.

The driver went limp and hit the sand like a bag of fetid laundry. He struggled to his feet, put his knife away and grasped the harnesses of the lead stallions.

The Monster whispered. The horses began fidgeting, lifting the driver up and down with each jerk of their mighty heads.

"Why are you seeking Aleron?" The Monster said.

Alvisor closed his eyes and thought hard. He concentrated on his tongue. It felt less controlled by the gem. He had gotten more energy reserves into grasp. Maybe...

"Speak, damn you! No one has the power to withstand The Traitor's Stone!"

"We—want—his—aid!" Alvisor said haltingly. "We —need—his—help—for—our—per—son—able—buddy —Roger!"

"Why?" The Monster's voice showed deep interest again. He glanced angrily at Roger. "Why does a Genie need a sorcerer's assistance? If it is because his magic will not work, I have blocked it, and have kept Aleron from blocking mine. How can *I* control the Genie Roger Lincoln? He is with you, so you must know how it is accomplished. Tell me!"

"Control the what?" Alvisor shouted with surprise.

"*I* ask the questions! *You* answer them!" The Monster roared.

"I remember," Alvisor said. "The Genie Roger!" He started laughing very coarsely.

"Stop it!" The Monster ordered. "You do not *chortle* under the mighty Traitor's Stone! You reply! *Stop it*! *Do it*! Spill your smelly guts! Now!"

"I can't help it!" Alvisor said with a giggle. "Roger, a Genie! Why do you imagine he's a Genie?"

"His fair features," The Monster said. "But, I am the clever master of unholy darkness who is asking the questions, you supposedly enraptured, effervescent jerk!"

"Did you ever think it was an accident?"

"An accident?" The Monster said, as though dazed. "He *isn't* a Genie!" He pulled himself as together as a psycho can almost get. "Then why is he seeking Aleron's dyspeptic aid? Speak!"

"He's from another world, here by freak of energy, and he wants to go back. Aleron can do it!" Alvisor said, like a frantic robot.

"*Another world*!" The Monster whispered. "I can kill Aleron, and conjure up a vision of this—Roger's—world. If I like its wonders, I can kill this—Roger—and take his place there. If I do not, I can still kill this—Roger—and have all of Aleron's magic tomes!" He returned his scrambled-egg brain's attention to Alvisor. "It is time you all conveniently died, in a tragic and mysterious manner!"

Alvisor flipped his beard double and grabbed the gem with its tips. He snapped the beard out, hurling the jewel at the coach.

The Monster turned and made a desperate grab, but missed. The Traitor's Stone shattered to dust against the side of the coach.

Alvisor struck The Monster on the back of the hood with his beard, then whacked him on the ass. The massive body ploughed into the coach and lay still on the floor. The hooded head stuck out the far door, the booted feet out the near.

The driver abandoned his useless efforts at stilling the wild horses, took out his knife and raced at Alvisor.

Roger felt his muscles relax. He fell to his knees, then leaped up and threw a punch at the driver. The driver dodged, raised his knife and jabbed at the top of Roger's head. Roger fell down to avoid the blade, his big feet striking the driver's legs. The driver collapsed on top of Roger and his knife sank into the sand beside Roger's right ear.

Wilkin and Alvisor scrambled to their feet. They hauled the driver off Roger and tossed him into the coach. They hastily pulled Roger out of the coach and flung the rapscallion driver in on top of The Monster.

Alvisor smacked the driver on the back of his odd, shiny head, with his beard tips, and the man went out like a defective light bulb.

The stallions could stand still no longer. They reared, snorting like loud locomotives, and bolted into movement. They circled the cul-de-sac, then raced out onto the main street, turning left, toward the distant front gates of the town.

"Come on!" Alvisor shouted. "When they wake up, they'll be hot on our tails!" He threw himself against the wagon, forcing it upright by riding it flat of his stomach.

Roger and Wilkin tossed the goods atop the wagon and they all plopped their frantic fannies on the bench. Alvisor reined the old mule forward, out of the cul-de-sac, and to the right, toward the gaping rear gates.

Chapter 7

I Play Crazy

"Our trusty mule appears to be bushed," Alvisor announced. "I'll stop now for a rest."

"Already?" Roger said. "But, we haven't gone—How far *have* we gone?"

Alvisor squinted myopically at the sun. "About ten miles, I'd say," he decided.

"That's ridiculous!" Roger said. "*Ten miles*! How can you judge that from looking at the sun?"

"Oh, I don't know as it's hard," Wilkin said. "Uncle Twiddley could tell a person's age by the burn marks on their legs."

"You may think it's ridiculous," Alvisor said, "but it works. And better than the brains of *some* people."

"He's got you pegged, Wilkin," Roger said.

"Or he's read your biography," Wilkin said.

"Probably your Family Tree," Roger said.

Alvisor laughed with Roger and Wilkin and reined the mule to a halt on the roadside.

"What about The Monster?" Roger said, looking nervously back down the road. "You said he'd be on our tails quick!"

"I *said*, when they come to, they'll be riding our rears," Alvisor said, with a chuckle. "He and his driver will be out, probably, four hours, with the raps I gifted them. The way those horses were galloping, it'll take The Monster several hours just to get back to Brown-Willow. By then, we'll be miles away from here, doing our best to keep our lead. Comforted?"

"Maybe," Roger said.

Alvisor climbed from the wagon and unhitched the mule. It was already asleep. He led the snoring animal to the grass in front of the left forest, then strode over, sat down beneath a tree, and passed out.

Roger jumped from the wagon and lifted Wilkin to the road. They strolled to a tree near Alvisor.

Wilkin propped himself against a large root. He dug into a pocket of his pants. After fumbling, he withdrew the pack of cigarettes and a metal box containing matches. He lit a fag and tossed the match on to the grass. He gazed down the straight road and began singing sexy songs lusciously to himself.

Roger leaned against the trunk and closed his eyes. Within five minutes, he was asleep. He had taken no rest since he had gone to work at the accounting firm the day before.

***

Wilkin was unable to sleep in the heat of the day. He had run out of choruses for his songs. So he was amusing himself by picking his nose and humping dirt into piles by the road. He jumped up, ran over, and jabbed a finger against Roger's ribs.

"What's wrong with you?" Roger grumbled.

"Funny noises!" Wilkin said. "Listen!"

Roger leaned forward and his forehead wrinkled. "You're correct," he said. "What do you think they are?"

"I can't quite place them," Wilkin admitted, with a red face.

"Let's see if Alvisor knows."

They trotted to the shaman's tree.

Roger shook the old man's shoulder. "Wake up, grandpa snoozer," he said.

Alvisor stiffened, fell onto his side, then onto his face, with his nose stuck in a Grommit burrow. He righted himself clumsily. "Explain your freakish selves!" he said angrily.

"We hear funny noises," Wilkin said. "Can you identify them?"

Alvisor peered at them suspiciously, but cocked his head to one side and listened. He leaped to his feet and ran for the wagon.

Alarmed, Roger and Wilkin charged after him.

On the way, Alvisor grabbed the mule's harness and jerked the startled, braying, complaining animal along. "Hurry up, sludge feet!" he shouted.

"What is it?" Roger quavered, darting his eyes up and down the shady, deserted road. "The Monster

here already?"

"Help me hitch up this damned mule!" Alvisor ordered. His voice was filled with urgency.

They fumbled for a minute or two, with Alvisor becoming more agitated. Finally, they untangled Wilkin from the halter, tracings and reins and got the mule hooked into place.

Alvisor shoved Wilkin onto the platform and climbed up to the bench.

Roger scrambled aboard and was seated just as the wagon began moving along the road. He held onto the edge of the bench between his legs. "What's making those curious sounds?" he demanded.

"*Bandits!*" Alvisor snapped. "No telling what crimes they're franchised to transact!"

The wagon rumbled faster along the road.

"I can see them!" Wilkin shouted.

Roger twisted around. Through the cloud of dust stirred up by the slow wagon, he saw what resembled three horsemen. They were galloping over a crown in the road and raising a dust cloud of their own.

Alvisor cracked the reins and the mule speeded up.

"Hold on tight, Wilkin," Roger said.

"They've sighted us!" Wilkin shouted from under the bench. "They're galloping faster our way!"

"Look out!" Roger warned.

There was a dead tree across the road, hidden in the shadows of the other trees. Alvisor did not see it in time, and Roger's shout was too late. The mule, however, reared, spun to its left on two hooves, and tried to run along beside the trunk. The wagon skidded to the right, thudded into the tree and rebounded onto its left side, pulling the mule over likewise. The animal laid there, limp and grateful for any opportunity to rest.

The trio was sent rolling toward the left forest. They jumped to their feet and began running. Behind them, the clopping of the bandits' horses increased in volume.

The distance from the old road to the forest had widened to nearly the length of a football field but the trio made it in about twenty-five, long terrified seconds.

Without hesitation, they plunged into the prickly shrubs and trees, not bothering to check for wild animals; they knew the truly dangerous beasts were already following them.

***

The trio crashed through thickets, tripped over vines and rebounded off tree after tree until they were finally forced to pause for rest. They stood puffing by a small tree in a large dip in the forest floor.

***

"I'll go see if the road is clear," Roger said, wondering where the courage was coming from and when it would peter out. He crept to the edge of the forest and crouched behind a growth of droopy purple bushes.

The three bandits were gathered around the capsized mule and wagon like undertakers around a rich man's corpse. The hulking leader was in the center of the red-habited group, right beside the booty.

Roger shinnied up a tree for a better seeing and hearing.

"What's this here we was chasing?" Boomed Quibb. He slapped a pink, cloth bag, with nose holes, over the head of his horse to quieten the beast. He was a huge black man.

"Ummm," Kwaggley said wisely. "It kinder resembles a wagon with food parcels and water skins, if ya knows what a feller does assuredly mean when he's really talking straight." He was eight feet of big-boned, sinewy, man-beast. His head was covered with coarse brown hair, as was his white face.

"You do sound serious!" Quibb exclaimed.

"Course," Kwaggley said. "A feller has to be when real serious heaps do present their selves to be perused."

"That hard gray thing there *might* be a old mule, Kwaggley," piped the third bandit. He was a fuzzy-haired, oriental-type. "To my hurted eyes, it's too unkindly ugly to be a mule, though." He screwed up his fat lips and spat a huge throat turd between his horse's flea chewed ears. The noble steed was not amused and shook the snot egg off its head.

"Be a might more sure if one of youse would get down and look at it close," Kwaggley said. He drew an amazingly long, and very sharp, sword from a sheath on the belt buckled around his absurdly muscled waist. Just a wee precaution against the motionless gray heap.

The oriental bandit left his saddle. He carefully inspected the wagon, its contents, and the gray lump. "Swell, damn!" he shouted. "T'is a wagon, goods, and *sort* of a mule!" He gazed admiringly at Kwaggley. "You sure got a real ripe eye!"

Kwaggley did not reply. His bloodshot lamps were as big as half dollars, his nostrils were flared and his forked tongue was trailing on his lap. "Was right!" he was finally able to shout. "There is some booze in one of them water bags! I knowed I scented some, five miles back!"

"Is me ears hearing true and well?" Quibb said, with a gasp. "Booze! But it cannot really be!" He sniffed hard, sounding like a vacuum cleaner with a mouse stuck in its nozzle. Then he smiled in a cretinous way. "But it is!" he rejoiced.

"A real crack find!" the third bandit proclaimed.

Kwaggley leaped from his saddle and sheathed his sword. He deftly flipped both the mule and the heavy wagon upright with his massive hands, kicking the bundle of goods back onto the bed at the same time. He handed the reins to Quibb. "We're gonna keep this odd treasure for ourselves, for blue socks, awful sure!" he vowed.

"You suppose this was being driven by what we was each sent after? To kill," the third bandit said.

Roger's grip on the tree slipped and he tumbled, flat on his back, into the bushes. Much to his credit, he did not cry out; he was too terrified. The perfidious bushes, however, made an unholy rustling.

"Whatever it is," Quibb shouted, "I want it!"

Kwaggley ran over like lightening and grabbed Roger out of the bushes.

Roger realized fighting Kwaggley would be like wrestling with a steam roller, so he tried every clever trick he could wring from his numb, terrified mind to gain a swift and happy release. "What are you doing?" he shouted. "Leave me alone! Hey! *Listen*! My mother's calling me!"

Kwaggley whistled his horse to him and tossed Roger, gut down, across its flanks. He took some ropes out of Quibb's saddlebags, tied Roger's wrists, and mounted the huge stallion, almost sitting on top of Roger. "We'll take fatty here to *Him*!" he crowed. "Maybe *He'll* give us a reward for letting *Him* have the kill!"

Roger recalled some of Alvisor's earlier words. An idea popped through his fear. "Hey, you guys got a Kidnap-Murder Franchise?" he screeched.

Kwaggley looked sad, but brightened up, showing

his cracked green teeth. "He's beat us *cool*," he told his cohorts grudgingly. "But we do *own* Thievery Tickets. We get to keep these goods, even if we do have to kick fatty loose!"

"We can't let it *go!*" Quibb said. "The Monster will rip our bodies fierce!"

"Yeah, sure," Kwaggley said, "but *Aleron's* the one who hands out the franchises. We break *his* rules, and even The Monster's *worst* won't compare to what *Aleron'll* commit upon us."

"What'll we do?" the third bandit squeaked. "Who's gonna tell *The Monster* we let his person go without killing *it*?"

"Nobody," Kwaggley said. "We just say they gave us the slip in the weeds and trees and all we got was their goods. Maybe he'll let us keep 'em."

"Bu—but, he can see through the air, over big distances," the third bandit said. "He'll know we lied."

"That's just reused gargle water," Kwaggley said. "*Aleron* can do that. All The Monster can do is sense where somebody is, if they's no further from him than six miles. Heard him mumble it once when he didn't know I was awake. We'll be fine. Was I always right before?"

Quibb smiled like a monster-sized infant. "You sure was!" he boomed.

"Yeah," the third bandit said. His flat chest puffed out with renewed confidence.

Kwaggley twisted around, untied the Earthman's wrists and shoved him off the horse.

Roger landed on his feet and stumbled backwards a few steps.

"Let's hie to the meeting place, boys," Kwaggley said. "I wants a ocean full o' that booze I found!"

Quibb removed the pink bag from his horse's head, causing the animal to awaken. He stowed the hood in his saddlebag.

They reined their overburdened steeds to the left, around the broken end of the fallen tree, and trotted down the road the direction the trio had been traveling.

Roger watched the mule, wagon and goods vanish over a rise in the road. He bravely flipped a double bird at where the bandits had been and raced back to Alvisor and Wilkin.

They were chanting for deliverance from evil, to Budda, a well known stage star. When they heard the foliage rustling, they stopped and pulled their hands from over their eyes.

"They're real gone, man," Roger said dourly. "So are our eats and our transportation." He snorted with anger. "Those bandits were sent after us by The Monster. He obviously turned around sooner than you expected, Nostradamus. I think they're going to meet him somewhere up the road. He must be coming this way, right now."

"That all was a foregone conclusion," Alvisor said, ignoring Roger's insult.

"What do we do?" Wilkin said.

Alvisor smiled like his mind had never been whole a day in his life. "We walk," he said, "until we reach a town up the road where we can buy some cheap horses. Even if it does mean a side trip and a delay."

"We can't use the road!" Wilkin protested. "The Monster will run us gooey!"

"Not if we jump out of the way," Alvisor said. "We'll hear him two minutes before we see him. Even *you* can jump into the bushes in that amount of time."

"Yeah," Wilkin said sarcastically. "Just like we heard him when he nearly creamed us on BrownWillow Road!"

Alvisor sneered disarmingly. "We'll be listening for him, this time," he said, "instead of to you raving about women." He led them through the twisty growths in the hollow and up onto the road.

"Was I raving about women?" Wilkin asked Roger.

"Your words were highly enthusiastic," Roger said, "but not rave-ish."

"Thank you," Wilkin said.

"Shut up," Alvisor said.

***

They had walked for about two hours when the left forest showed a tiny break. Alvisor grabbed Roger's shoulder and pointed out a big column of white smoke.

It was rising from behind a low ridge of rough yellow rock situated in the break. The trio halted.

"You know what that is, Roger?" Alvisor said.

"Sure," Roger said, "smoke."

"No, ass. I mean, yes," Alvisor said. "But it happens to be coming from a campfire. And that may mean—"

Roger paled so artfully he could have blended himself into newly fallen snow. "The bandits!" he blurted.

"And *The Monster*!" Wilkin squeaked.

"Very possibly," Alvisor said. "There are many alternate routes from BrownWillow through the forests. This may be why we haven't seen the roach coach. This could be our lucky break!"

"*Lucky*?" Roger said, obviously preparing to flee. "How?"

"We need transportation," Alvisor said. "They have our overpriced transportation. We transfer ownership of our transportation back to us."

"You're crazy!" Roger said.

"That's what most people think," Alvisor said. "But, old Alvisor ain't crazy. That's how come I've been around so long, boy, I *play* crazy."

"Yeah!" Wilkin said. "Well, if you play with those bandits and The Monster, you won't be crazy any more. No, sir, you'll we wide-throated dead!"

Roger agreed loudly and with considerable vulgarity.

"Only if we make a mistake," Alvisor said. "If that happens, you won't return home, Roger. So, I don't think we'll make any mistakes."

"You're damned right we won't!" Wilkin shouted. "Because we're gonna keep walking down this safe, friendly road until we find that town where we can buy some damned horses!"

"Just as I thought," Alvisor said, "cowards. The both of you. I'll tell you what," he interrupted himself cleverly, "let's sneak over there and spy around. It if seems too dangerous, we'll keep on walking. Does that sound fair?"

"I guess so," Roger said reluctantly. "Is that okay with you, Wilkin?"

"No!" Wilkin shouted. "But you'll commit that wit-less sin anyway, and like an ass head, I'll go shambling along!"

They left the road and crossed a patch of scarlet weeds to the ridge. It ran parallel to the road and was almost too steep to climb. They prayed for a few moments, then crawled carefully to the top. Below, the forest receded in an oval, creating a dusty, infertile clearing. It was strewn with rocks and a few boulders. It was also littered with the three bandits. They were sprawled around a bonfire like they were expecting the raid. There were paper wrappers near the fire, showing they had callously eaten some of the trio's food. One of the water bags was uncorked and empty beside Kwaggley.

"It don't look too bad," Alvisor said.

"Too bad!" Roger hissed. "Look at them! They have their eyes open as wide as full moons! Once we leave this rock, they'll see us from any angle we approach! They might even hear us now! And, what about *The Monster*! They were going to meet him! Probably here! He might be near here, right now!"

"Do you see him?" Alvisor said. "Not even Aleron knows invisibility. So The Monster ain't here. They're probably double crossing him, or he ain't showed up yet. If so, we'd best get our stuff back quick before he comes! Do you have a knife, Roger?"

Roger stared at the old man. "All I have is one pocket and it's full of pocket watch," he said.

"I got one," Wilkin said. He tugged a sheathed dagger out of the left front pocket of his slacks and held it up like show and tell in school.

"Good," Alvisor said, like a doting father. He turned cheerily to Roger. "The mule and wagon, with most of the food and water still on it, are to the left of those far trees. One of us will go to it. The other two will distract the bandits from the camp. The guy with the knife cuts the mule and wagon loose and meets the other two down the road a ways. Got that?"

"Yes," Roger said sourly. "Who does what?"

"The way I see it," Alvisor said. "Wilkin, being the shortest, should get the wagon. He can sneak up to it because the grass there is far taller than he is."

"I was mortally afraid of that," Roger said, with a groan. "That means you and I distract the friendly, neighborhood, psychotic bandits."

"Right," Alvisor said, as if they were off to a picnic. "Get toddling, Wilkin."

Wilkin appeared unhappy for a moment, but slipped the dagger into his pocket and crept away to the left.

"Now what?" Roger asked nervously.

A strange expression took control Alvisor's face. He advanced upon Roger, moving faster than a leaf in a hurricane.

***

A short time later, Alvisor slipped around the bandits' camp the in same direction Wilkin had. The old quack bore a bundle under one arm. When he reached a rock large enough to hide him, he raised the bundle over his head.

When Roger sighted the bundle, he raced down the ridge, around its right end, and past the bonfire. He was running so fast, the wind friction gave him a nice, golden-brown tan. Halfway along the trip, he grabbed a peekaroo at the bandits, but was too terrified to make sense of what he saw. He slid around behind Alvisor, kicking up a shower of stones and a cloud of dust with his shoes. "No good, *damn you!*" he said, gasping for breath. He angrily snatched the bundle from the Magus and began dressing. "They didn't follow me!"

"There goes my genius plan," Alvisor said dejectedly. As he searched his brain for a shiny new scheme, he peeped over the rock. "Well, I'll be licentious!" he said. "The closer we get to them, the more petrified they look!"

"What?" Roger said. He pulled on his pajama top and buttoned it. "Lemmie see!"

"I'll go check," Alvisor said. "Be ready to flee in desperate horror."

"Already gone," Roger said wryly.

Alvisor crept around the rock, holding his beard like a whip.

Kwaggley was staring at the magician, but the fearsome bandit did not register any recognition of the conjurer's existence.

Alvisor tapped the third bandit on top of the head. "Hardest waste rock I ever seen," he said, with humiliating relief. "Come and gleefully gape."

Roger cautiously joined the magician. He remained three feet away from each bandit but looked them over curiously, like a crab shoving its eye stalks at a possible morsel of food. "They look terrified," he said.

"What's this here?" Alvisor said. He knelt creakily near the bonfire. "Somebody's drawn a spiffy picture in the dirt."

It was a gloved hand grasping a globe which featured the word HackHell between the ends of the fingers and thumb.

Roger tried to scuff the picture out with the toe of his shoe but it was glazed into the earth, as eternal as the justifiably petrified bandits. "It's The Monster," he peeped. "He's been here already and turned them into unseemly lawn geeks. This ugly logo is his twisted calling card."

"When you're right, you're obscenely right," Alvisor said. "Let's see if they have any glod, then meet up with Wilkin."

"You see if they have any free glod," Roger said. "I'm getting my nice round ass out of here!"

Alvisor did not fail to stick close to Roger's nice round ass.

***

When Wilkin, the mule and the wagon were not among the tethered horses of the bandits, Alvisor and Roger headed for the road. They negotiated the maze of trees and vines surprisingly swiftly and met Wilkin just as he reached the highway.

Wilkin was leading the mule by the reins.

He turned around and smiled broadly.

Then Wilkin smiled. "No! Yes! It's the Naked Wonder and his faithful Geriatric Companion!" he hailed. "What took you so long?"

"Checking them bandits," Alvisor said. "The Monster petrified them."

"Oh," Wilkin said. "I thought they'd zonked out on

the booze I put into one of the water bags. You think The Monster is up the road, somewhere, waiting for us?"

"If not," Alvisor said, as he seated himself on the wagon, "he's beelining it to Aleron's, and we gotta try to beat him there in order to save Aleron's magical neck. Or Roger, here, will never get back to his no doubt, pitiful hole-in-the-wall home!"

Chapter 8

Thwack! Thwack!

"This is the place you described, master!" the driver shouted. He reined in the stallions and kicked down the brake control.

"You are the only moron I can almost trust," The Monster telepathed.

"Thank you, master!"

The coach shuddered to a stop, the left door flipped open and the steps folded down.

The forests lining the road from BrownWillow had come to an abrupt end, revealing rolling fields of orange weeds to the left, and a huge canyon to the right.

The Monster de-coached and motioned to the driver. "I left their mule and wagon intact so they will ride headlong into this ingenious trap. It will not take long to set this grisly snare. Be here, prepared to resume our travels, upon my return."

"Only a fool would disobey, master!"

"This is why I warned you!"

"Bless you, master!"

The Monster strode across the weeds parallel and

close to the edge of the left forest. He quickly came to a towering, malformed shape covered by vines from the forest. He removed his gloves, tucking them into a pocket of his habit. He raised his arms and sent fire into the thick vines, incinerating them and revealing the great shape.

**

Thwack! Thwack!

The Monster paused at the edge of the road.

Thwack! Thwack!

"Driver! Where are you?" he shouted angrily.

"Here, master! In the other forest!"

"What are you doing?"

"Beating myself as I promised, master!"

Thwack! Thwack!

"You're early," The Monster observed.

"Yes, master! I wished to get it over with quickly. Forgive me!"

"Come here!"

"Shall I bring the stick, master?"

"Only your degenerate self!" The Monster said, pulling his gloves from his pocket and putting them on. He entered the coach and the door snapped shut. "Damn!" he muttered. The door flopped open, the steps folded up properly, and the door slammed closed.

The driver trotted out of the right forest a little way down the road. He stood beside the left door. His face was rather flushed and he was looking self satis-

fied.

"The spell will commence after we pass beyond the canyon," The Monster said. "Mount, driver, you have enjoyed yourself enough for one day!"

Chapter 9

The Broken Break Break

"What's making that grinding noise ahead?" Roger asked, with a nervous smile. "All the bandits in existence?"

"We're out of Bandit Land," Alvisor said.

***

A cloud of dust appeared over the forest to their left. It grew bigger and bigger.

Alvisor slowed the mule, then he stopped it.

"What could raise so much dust?" Roger said. He anxiously watched the cloud getting larger. Not nearer, just eerily larger.

"Lots of things," Wilkin said, from a pocket of Alvisor's robe.

"Like Magic Devices what are out of control!" Alvisor shouted. "And that's what's over there!"

Roger strained his eyeballs and, yes! Egad! There was some—*Thing*—in the dirt cloud! But he could discern none of its, no doubt revolting, features. "Will it bother us?" he said.

"There ain't no way of telling yet," Alvisor said. He

directed the wagon further down the lonely road.

Wilkin hunkered deeper into Alvisor's spacious pocket.

***

The grinding became a steady noise.

***

The earth began trembling.

To Roger, the sound toward which they were reluctantly traveling, was like a locomotive steaming over sheet metal laid across The Grand Canyon.

To Alvisor and Wilkin, the din was simply horrible!

***

The forests petered out. Rolling fields of orange weeds lay to their left. A canyon yawned impolitely to their right.

In spite of their ever nearing the gigantic shape, its features remained obscured by the gloomy cloud of dust. It was like watching a monster through a dirty window, knowing the monster was searching for *you*.

Roger was so frightened he was clinging to Alvisor like it was their wedding night.

Wilkin, of course, was still in the old man's pocket, smoking one turkey flavored cigarette after another.

***

The orange weeds thinned to bare brown earth.

***

A giant trench yawned obscenely between the road and the left forest. It was about one hundred feet across and about that many deep.

There was empty space on both sides of the trio. And the road led directly toward the rumbling, clanking *Thing* which lurked in the cloud of billowing dust.

"It *is* a machine!" Roger shouted, in relief, upon hearing the clanking sounds. "That's good!"

"What do you mean?" Alvisor croaked, with disbelief. He reined the mule to a halt and watched the indistinct Thing expanding the trench at the left side of the road. In a few minutes, the machine would inconsiderately tear the road in half, making it impassable.

"It isn't a monster," Roger said.

"That makes it worse!" Wilkin said, with a sob. He tossed a glowing fag butt out of the pocket. "It ain't under even no one's *evil* control!"

"Then how's it run?" Roger scoffed. "Pure luck? Or maybe its spring hasn't wound down yet?"

"Maybe you would like to go shut it off?" Alvisor said. "Magic made it and magic runs it. I thought Aleron turned it off, for good, twenty years ago. I guess he only managed to stun it."

Stun! Roger thought. You stun an animal, not a machine! Not on Earth. Or even Mars, probably. "But, I'm not on Mars," he mumbled, "And they stun them machines here! What'll we do?" he said. "Can it see?

Will it hurt us? Does it eat? Us? With salt? Or chives?"

"And a hundred tons of rocks and dirt," Alvisor said. "But, if we move fast, we might be able to get past it before it can chew the road in half and come after us. And we might out run it to town!"

"Let's get going, then!" Wilkin screamed. His booted feet were sticking out of Alvisor's baggy pocket. "Before I become an albino from fear!"

Alvisor grasped the reins more tightly and magically snapped his beard tips against the mule's wrinkled rump. The disgruntled animal jumped and brayed angrily, but the wagon rumbled faster down the road, creaking and crackling.

***

The dusty machine became the only thing on the left horizon. Its noise began vibrating the wagon and the trio.

***

As they came alongside the machine, their nearness enabled them to see it through the flying dust. They gaped at the horror like monkeys watching a chainsaw-wielding robot.

The machine looked like a dozen ice cream scoops on the ends of flexible metal tentacles, attached to a dozen tree limb chippers arranged, back to back, on a steel platform, with large, sporty black wheels. Dirt and rocks were scooped into the chipper blades, ground to dust and discharged high into the air through the huge, curving blower conduits.

Alvisor snapped his beard to speed up the mule. But not soon enough. Steely eyes opened on some of the blower conduits. They fixed their gaze on the trio. After a moment, the eyes got a message to the rest of the machine and it began rolling toward the trio. As the evil machine moved, it gathered speed.

"Here it comes!" Wilkin screamed, with unabashed and enviable despair. He pulled his head back into Alvisor's pocket and started reciting his last will and testament as recorded on a wall of the bedroom of his tiny, but precocious, brick home.

Roger twisted awkwardly around. The machine was hot on their tails, raising a cloud of dust behind their own. "Get this buggy going!" he urged.

"I *am!*" Alvisor groused. He snapped his beard. The tired old mule's only response was a resentful stare over its gray, bony shoulder. Alvisor cursed and slapped the mule's flank with one of Roger's heavy feet. The startled, angry beast leaped forward, jerking the complaining wagon faster after it.

"The machine's speeded up!" Roger warned.

Alvisor raised Roger's foot again. The mule must have sensed what was coming. It swished its long tail in defense. Alvisor wiped hair from his eyes.

Roger yelped.

Sad Wilkin started whining.

The superannuated mule snorted in rage but managed to run faster.

Just as they were making headway, the harness broke and the wagon fork split along its short length, releasing the ancient mule. The overjoyed animal performed a model u-turn and fled, stiff-legged, but in a sure-footed fashion, down the side of the canyon.

The wagon continued along the road at a fast clip. After about a hundred feet, there were thousands of ear-drum-hurting creaks and snaps and the conveyance splintered. Vibration fatigue is what the technicians on Earth would call it.

One minute, they were hurtling along at nearly eighteen wild miles per hour, the next, they were sitting atop a pile of overrated kindling and marginal foodstuff.

"Damn! Damn! Damn!" Roger shouted. He jumped up like a jack in the box, only he jiggled more. "*Come on*! Get off your laggard bottoms and *move*!"

Wilkin rolled out of the magician's pocket and leaped to his feet.

Alvisor kicked part of the wagon fork off his chest and rose like a bent over sapling suddenly released.

Within split seconds, the trio was fleeing forward down the road. But the machine was catching up from their left. It scooped in and spat out the remains of the wagon and food supplies without even thinking of slowing.

Roger's heart skipped a beat as they crested a hill. The road ended at a steep cliff. The machine had already proudly accomplished its dirty work there. Roger's heart skipped another beat. There was a narrow strip of earth where the new trench ended and the canyon began.

Wilkin kept tripping, stumbling and rolling in front of Roger and Alvisor. They lifted him off the ground by his arms, like parents with a child, raced across the break, and darted into some very tall bushes along the left side of the next section of the road.

The machine followed, but the break was not strong enough to support all that magically perverted metal. The sides of the flimsy land bridge crumbled, and the machine slid to a stop; its sporty, ebony wheels spinning in the amused, mocking air. The whirring behemoth teetered nauseatingly for several seconds, then toppled over the canyon side of the break. It clawed desperately at the land bridge with its scoops, but only succeeded in pulling loose huge chunks of dirt and rocks after itself.

A terrible stripping of gears and rending of metal echoed throughout the canyon. Then silence fell.

The weary, relieved travelers struggled out of the bushes, warily approached the canyon rim, and looked at a black speck below.

Alvisor kicked some dirt at the pile of twisted, inert metal. "Damned freaked out steel!" he said.

"What was it?" Roger said.

"A garden flower planter," Alvisor said. "But the dippy magician who conjured it tossed in too much power and it got enlarged and warped. All it would do was separate towns to keep people from traveling between them. And it would try to kill those who left the towns." He scratched his head thoughtfully. "From the looks of these trenches, the machine was running wild for only a few hours. Aleron will have to fill them in, like last time, so trade can continue."

"What happened to the guy who bungled the machine?" Wilkin asked.

"He got caught up in the blades as soon as he switched the monstrosity on," Alvisor said. He dumped Wilkin's cigarette ashes out of his pocket. "Shows you what kind of a loony, defect-head he was."

"Yeah," Roger said. "Yeah."

"What's this?" Wilkin asked, with charming innocence. He was standing in the center of the dusty road.

"What?" Roger said, as he and Alvisor joined the dwarf.

"I should have known!" Alvisor said. "It figures! We knew The Monster was probably ahead of us. We should have assumed he'd try to keep us from reaching Aleron first."

"*The Monster* made this pretty picture?" Wilkin said. "How?"

"Burned it into the earth with psychic energy," Alvisor said. "Since he's the one who turned the machine on, he probably knows it didn't kill us and, no doubt, he's also brought the Magic Garden back to life! We've got to walk through *that*, and it ain't going to be no, fancy-pants, hose-down, dance!"

Chapter 10

The Galloping Gobblers

"What place *is* this?" Roger asked angrily.

There was sparse grass on either side of the road and the earth was rife with ruts and dips and hills. Black rock columns insulted the sky with their pointing. Tall, white, human-hand-shaped plants kept grasping at the trio.

The trench was beyond the plants and columns on the left and the great canyon was beyond the plants and columns on the right.

"Why, it's The Plain of Palms, of course," Alvisor said. "Part of the machine magician's Magic Garden." He snapped one of the plants with his beard to keep the palm away. "I told you we'd be coming to it. But, I didn't think it would be so soon!"

"Why do they insist on pinching *me*?" Roger said. He was resentfully rubbing sore spots on his sides and thighs.

"And on cuddling *me*?" Wilkin said. He slapped a palm away from his thigh, then started back toward it, then ran and hugged one of Roger's knees.

Roger was tired.

Alvisor was stuck for an answer. Then, as if a bird had soiled him. "Why! That's it! We knowed all along!" he said. "There are factions of them Palms. One is The Pinchers. One is The Cuddlers. Them Pinchers are, by nature, nasty brutes that prey on fat women." He eyed Roger apologetically. "Most of the time. And them Cuddlers, there, rubbing Wilkin, are kind and very friendly."

"Annoying, slippery and cruelly seductive!" Wilkin rasped, in a soft, sexually aroused voice. He ran to the center of the road to escape his latest fondlers. "Let's cut out of this nightmare of pale patties!" he begged.

***

The waving Palms slowly thinned, but the trio found themselves face to face with a grove of Monster Palms, each twenty feet high and seventeen feet wide.

Since the canyon was to the trio's right and the trench to their left, behind the plants, there was no way to go but along the road, between the Monster Palms.

"And there are Monster Palms," Alvisor said, finishing his lecture on HackHell Magical Flora, "that smash you dead and greasy on the corpse strewn road. Unless you moves quicker than a greased fart!"

Like the punishing hand of a gargantuan father, the first Monster Palm slapped at them with air whistling speed.

The trio fled down the road with their heels pounding their backs. Each time a Monster Palm hit home

behind them, the ground rumbled like a priest without a congregation, they bounced into the air, came down hard, and continued running.

Roger felt like he was on an out-of-control roller coaster ride but without the convenience and security of a coach. He was almost ready to toss up his cookies when the last Monster Palm impacted behind them.

The road ceased shaking like a fat man's belly, silence descended, and they ran into a huge, natural, gray-rock tunnel. They stopped to catch their breath. Mainly because they deftly tripped over each other and fell down. There was barely enough light from the ends of the tunnel for them to see each other.

"So what?" Alvisor demanded, to unspoken accusations and slurs. "So The Monster made us scream through a Monster Palm Grove! So I couldn't counteract his magic in them! So they almost killed us! So long!" he added, as he recalled a bit of unspeakable lore concerning the Great Rock Tunnel.

Roger and Wilkin chased after the manic magician.

"All right," Roger admitted, though he cleaned his big mouth out later with top soil, "nobody's perfect. Everybody makes mistakes. Everybody has a right to be wrong. No need for you to desert us in our sad hour of need in this godforsaken Tunnel!"

Alvisor halted. The dim light revealed his utter, painful amazement. "Desert, boy!" he shouted. "Who's deserting? I'm wildly fleeing for my miserable, shitty life! They're in here! With their wicked eyes glinting! Their huge teeth shining! And their long, sharp finger-nails tapping out a boogie-woogie death march!" He swished his tail and was off again.

Wilkin had exercised his dwarfish protection mea-sure; he had willed himself unconscious. He was hang-ing from Roger's right shoulder with his tiny fingers as tight as bent nails.

A Freak Wind suddenly sprang up. It batted little Wilkin against Roger's side. Roger skidded to a stop and irately hit the Wind with a stick he discovered in his pajama bottoms.

The Freak Wind huffed with indignation, raised a blue umbrella over its round, bald head and ran, puff-ing, down the Tunnel the way the trio had entered.

"What *are* they?" Roger said to the Magus. He had caught up with Alvisor and was running beside him.

Wilkin had unwillingly awakened at the sound of Roger's voice.

Roger grabbed Wilkin by the back of the collar with his right hand and held the dwarf high up in front of him, like a wild-eyed, protective charm.

"Desert, you accused!" Alvisor said, with a wail. His beard was bobbing as he spoke. It was sticking straight out in front of him, being used as a double tipped lance. "Dessert's what we'll be, if we don't van-ish from this Tunnel like a paycheck in a whore store! They're in here! Freckled damn, they're in here!"

"What *are* they, rascal?" Roger shouted. He held Wilkin over his terrified eyeballs. They were of no real use anyway, as glazed and enlarged as they had become. He was clinging to the cuff of the Magus's flapping sleeve so they would not get separated.

"Must be cars!" Wilkin raved, with one half of his fourth of a mind, even though he had never seen or heard of them before. "Cars and Vans and Trains, all hard and loud and hungry for our lives! They'll sup on us with their massive, slavering, loose lipped, multiple, foul smelling mouths!"

Wilkin was shaking like an out of control jackhammer. Roger could no longer use him as a vision shield. He jammed the dwarf under his right arm and drew nearer to the speeding Magus. His sad eyes were forced to return to their normal shape and texture. At the end of the dismal Great Rock Tunnel, he saw whirling reflections of sparkling sunlight, a giant, sinister, amorphous shape, and maybe a tasty custard pie, or two. He stopped and licked the top of a pie setting on a boulder in the center of the floor.

"*No! Don't!*" Alvisor warned, with desperation. "It's a cruel, depraved ruse! A *trap!*—A peace offering?"

"The beginning of our promised, free, sumptuous, man meal!" The booming, unearthly voice echoed througout the accursed tunnel.

"Sorry," Roger babbled, "this is *our* delicacy!" He balanced the custard pie atop his dizzy head, grabbed

Alvisor by the beard, and dashed to the left, around the boulder, toward the end of the Tunnel. Wilkin was still under his right arm.

Roger and Alvisor darted around the hulking shape. Five shaggy throwbacks with glowing red faces galloped up from the sides of the gray Tunnel. They thoughtlessly snatched the pie off Roger's airy head with their cerise radiating fingernails.

The towering dark form fell apart. It was, in sinful truth, revealed to be more of the crude, hairy beasts. They grasped at the trio, their fingernails clacking sickeningly together with each bungling attempt. They began chasing the trio.

"What *are* they, damn it?" Roger persisted.

"The Galloping Gobblers!" Alvisor shouted. "I've heard of them all my curious life! They can be formed from the rocks in this blighted Tunnel, with sufficient magic! The Monster had it! They'll slurp us alive and wear our clothes! *Flee faster*!"

"My body's four feet ahead of my toes now!" Roger complained.

"You ain't fast enough yet!" Alvisor squalled. "Your pointy chin has to wear a groove in the cold stone floor!"

"Do something!" Roger pleaded.

"I am!" Alvisor snapped. He was whipping himself on the hip with his red beard tips, causing unearthly sharp booms to echo in the Tunnel.

"Use a spell to save us!" Roger demanded angrily.

"Give me one!" Alvisor blubbered. "My head; it's all blank!"

Four Gobblers were passing the trio on the left, four on the right.

"They're gonna cut us off!" Roger warned. He swung wildly at the nearest Gobbler with Wilkin, using the distraught dwarf like a fear stiffened baseball bat.

"Arruuggaalaahh!" the hairy horror screamed. "I done been touched by a *dwarf*! Contaminated! Uncleaned!" It flopped to the floor, flat of its red face, and disintegrated in a bright green flame, causing a sound like a bullet ricocheting off metal.

"Dwarf!"

"Dwarf!"

"Dwarf!"

"Dwarf!"

The Gobblers passed the hideous word back to their cohorts. They skidded to a stop and stood shaking in random order. There was a horrific buzzing, then they flared out of existence, with brilliant emerald flames, making tinny popping sounds like flash bulbs in an insane series connection until not one vile Gobbler survived.

Roger herded his grateful companions out of the Tunnel of terror. The dusty road now ran between fields of towering grass.

Chapter 11

Like the Blade of a Guillotine

"The Traitor's Stone must have refreshed the old magician's memory, in small part. Magic has assisted them. But it has been mostly unnatural, naughty luck," The Monster rumbled, from the comfort of his coach.

"Yes, master," the driver said, from his hard seat.

They were stopped on the road between fields of tall grass.

"That luck will not last much longer. What form shall the second part of my spell assume?"

The driver remained morosely silent. He realized the master did not expect even a stupid answer from him. He just wished the master would order the coach on. The Cold Spell which the master had enjoined and dispatched back toward the worrisome men, was awfully close to dispatching the driver, as well, in spite of the heat of the sun on his head and back. The wind grew colder and he pulled his hood closer around his face.

"Driver!"

"Yes, master!"

"There is a cave near here, in the grass field on your left. Find it. Go into it and place your palms against the rear wall. Do not move them until I say!"

"Yes, master." He hastened down and vanished into the tall, wind stirred grass. As he moved, he grew warmer. The grass also cut down some of the wind's bite.

"Keep straight, you imbecile!" The Monster roared telepathically. "It lies right in front of you!"

A hump of rock, covered with earth and grass, merged with the field and the driver stumbled into the specified cave. It was pitch dark even though the sun was still up. But it was warmer here than in the windswept grass. He struck his feet and hands on outcroppings but found the rear of the gloomy cave quickly. With reluctance, he placed his hands to the cool stone, as instructed, and waited nervously.

The master was not known for his mercy. If he were going to cast some horrible kind of spell to trap the men, using him as a conduit, it would probably hurt. He gritted his teeth and took a deep breath.

The cave vibrated for a few seconds. A red glow misted around him, coursed hotly through his hands, and into the stone. The wall grew nearly too hot to touch.

The cave shook violently once.

"Who wakens Zukove?" a thunderous, cruel voice roared. "Zukove must sleep! Zukove will kill *you*!"

"Master!" the driver screamed. "May I leave now?

Please!"

A foggy shape materialized at the left side of the cave.

The driver felt this eerie figure was very distressingly too near.

The shape was malformed and huge.

More massive, the driver thought, than even the horrible master.

The form was slavering loudly.

The driver was shaking so hard with terror, he could not keep his hands against the hot wall.

"Return!" The Monster telepathed.

The driver screamed with wild relief and fled the cave like a fish from an electrified net.

The ghostly figure darted after the driver but came up short at the cave entrance.

***

The driver thrashed out of the last of the tall grass. The coach was as still as death. Only the horses were twitching. He stood by the curtained window. He was still breathing hard and shaking from terror.

"What did you observe?" The Monster asked.

"Zu—Zukove's ghost!" the driver rasped. "It tried to kill me!"

"Excellent! They will be unable to continue beyond this point without resting in shelter for the night. They will use the cave. And Zukove will use them!"

"But, master," the driver said, "they cannot *see* the

accursed cave!"

"Mount, driver, I shall attend to that piddly detail!"

The driver took his seat and grabbed the reins in both hands. He did not want the stallions to move the coach while the master plied his magic. He would be punished if they did.

The curtain on the left window snapped up. Red flames snaked out of the coach, and the grass leading to the cave was incinerated. A cold wind swirled away the fine gray ashes as The Monster magically erased all evidence of his fire. The curtain rolled down like the blade of a guillotine.

"On, slothful driver! We waste time!"

Chapter 12

The Haunted Cave

"How long to that town?" Wilkin asked wearily.

An unseasonably cold wind had sprung up, whipping the grass into dizzying waves on both sides of the road. In spite of the heat from the afternoon sun, the travelers were shivering.

"We'll make it in about four hours," Alvisor said.

"Can we stop some where soon, get out of this *cold* for a while, and take a nap?" Wilkin begged.

"All right," Alvisor said. "*If* we find shelter before the town."

Roger plodded dully behind Wilkin and Alvisor. He was unable to keep his attention from the hypnotic motions of the grass. He was hungry and angry at his situation. They had come afoul so much trouble, he was almost ready to give up the journey to the real magician and resign himself to living on this backwoods, mud ball of a planet.

He sighed distractedly and sat down on the dirt road. He watched Wilkin and Alvisor growing smaller with distance. He half chuckled. "They haven't even noticed I'm not with them," he mumbled. "Probably won't realize it for another ten minutes." The hypnotic motions of the grass fully captured his attention. He thought about his apartment. Warm and cozy, it was. Dry. Warm. And *very* cozy.

***

Roger stood up in his drab living room. A steaming cup of coffee, and a plate of sandwiches, were on the blue plastic coffee table. The aroma of the coffee made his mouth water.

He shuffled across the red linoleum with the white Q design, to his nineteen inch color television and tuned in the Jack Dargon Variety Show. He settled into his yellow vinyl easy chair and decided he would never leave its nest-like softness. Alvisor and Wilkin appeared mistily before him.

Wilkin looked frightened.

The shaman appeared sad. Worried. Like he had lost all of his neurotically beloved glod. "Come on!" he said urgently. He tugged on Roger's right hand. "You can't stay here, you'll freeze!"

Freeze, Roger thought, how can I freeze? My apartment's always warm. He freed his hand from Alvisor's grasp and reached for his coffee. The cup and pot dissolved. So did the plate of sandwiches and the table.

Wilkin was trying to hold Roger's eyes open. "Please stay awake, Roger!" he pleaded. "We can't stay here!

Please get up!"

Roger laughed and pushed the dwarf away. He yawned. "I wanna sleep," he mumbled. A slap to his pale cheek brought him to his senses. He allowed himself to be pulled to his feet. He stumbled, then began walking beside Alvisor and Wilkin without their help.

***

To the left of the weary travelers, the tall waving grass gave way to a small clearing, revealing a cave in a chunk of earth and grass covered rock. Roger led Alvisor and Wilkin inside. It was mercifully warmer here because the wind was blocked out.

Roger felt his way along the dark cave, sat on the floor and leaned against the right wall.

Alvisor and Wilkin laid down near each other and fell immediately asleep.

Roger curiously found himself too nervous to sleep. He decided to explore the cave. As he ran his hand along the right wall, it slipped into a crevice and got stuck. He did not want his pals to know his shame, so he tried self extrication. He placed his feet against the wall and drew his knees down until his legs were straight. This raised his bottom off the floor. His hand slipped free and he flew against Alvisor's chest, waking him.

"If you're no longer tired enough to sleep," Alvisor observed testily, "you could take a walk!"

"Sorry," Roger said, as ingenuously as possible. He

stepped restlessly into the sun. The wind had ceased and it was less cold.

He walked across the dusty clearing and sat at the side of the road. He propped an elbow on a knee, his chin on a palm and, disgusted, stared into the distance.

***

Roger awoke with a pig snort. The sun was filling the sky with pickle greens and rough neck reds. He pried his hand from his chin and wrestled his arm straight. He was lucky the wind had not begun blowing again. He would have died of exposure in his sleep.

***

Roger slipped into the semi dark cave.

Alvisor was asleep with Wilkin cuddled in his arms.

Roger thought the Magus resembled a gross child with a teddy bear.

Wilkin-teddy was not thrilled by the situation. In fact, his little eyes were bloodshot and his tiny ears were pale. "Am I glad you're back!" he said, with a grunt. He was prying at Alvisor's arms. "I thought sure I wouldn't get help before I croaked!"

Roger bent close to get a better look at the grip Alvisor had on the dwarf.

"This bearded fetus has slid into the gummy ichor of his subconscious memories of his abnormal, tear jerker childhood. And I have cruelly been appropriated as the symbol of his favorite security object. I'm lying in fear that my tissue-paper-thin ribs will get crushed by the landslide hold this demented spell fumbler has fastened onto me. *Help me, damn you!*"

Roger thought Wilkin's discourse sounded uncharacteristic of the dwarf, but decided the unusual circumstances probably warranted it. He grabbed Alvisor's coarse beard and began to slap the magician to a waking state with its forked tips.

"The shame of it is, my terminally laconic and marginally obese friend," Wilkin screamed, at the top of his tiny lungs, filling the cave with spooky echoes, "the pain is making me sound twistedly educated, and unutterably intelligent! *Help me, you morbid, wet-bottomed fatness!*"

Alvisor dimly heard the distraught plea of some needful being. He snapped erect ten seconds before he was awake, dumped the indignant dwarf on the rough stone floor, and chanted:

"When some bedeviled beggar needs,

"it's Alvisor's magic for which he pleads!

"I'll turn his monstrous woes to sod

"for one small sack of gleaming glod!"

The red fires in Wilkin's rolling eyes convinced the Magus he had better find protection from the hot vengeance about to be wreaked upon him for some unintended transgression he must have committed in his somnambulistic state.

"A teddy bear am I!" Wilkin roared, with a voice which sounded like it belonged to nine feet of green, drooling cruelty. "I'll show you who's a teddy bear!"

Roger's eyelids pasted themselves against his milky forehead.

Alvisor's beard lost its vulgar curls.

"With cute, button-eyes and fuzzy, felt-tipped nose, no doubt!" Wilkin raved. He fidgeted beneath his shirt and pulled out a Wedsell dislodging knife. It's multi-folding blade clacked out to its full eight foot length and its eight pronged tip touched Alvisor's sweat-beaded forehead. Wilkin came to his senses. He squeaked like a mouse stumbling upon a convention of starving cats, and dropped the knife. "Where'd such mischief come from?" he stammered. "Ain't no room in *my* small body for such mischief!" He jumped on the knife. With loud metallic clicks, and soft slicing sounds, it retracted into a column of steel just ten inches long. "Who's is this?" he said. He held the dislodger out to Alvisor. "Yours?"

"This must be Zukove's Cave!" Alvisor whispered. "Where awful acts were committed with knives before the world was civilized!" He slapped the ugly implement out of Wilkin's trembling hand. "That's Zukove's Haunted Torture Knife!" he said. "The crimes he used to commit with that made macho demons weep!" He blanched. "That wicked metal had control of all of our peewee minds! Let's get gone from here!"

The cave vibrated violently.

The trio fell to their knees. A bitter cold, and inconsolable fear, shivered them.

"You awaken Zukove! You anger Zukove! You should fear Zukove! Zukove will chill you! Zukove will kill you!"

The hulking shape ghosted into being at the mouth of the cave. It was slavering more loudly than when its equally unenthusiastic guest had been the driver of The Monster's coach.

"You gaily think Zukove don't adore the deep slumber of his forced retirement from his godforsaken life! You think Zukove is kind when you rakishly disturb him?"

Roger seized Wilkin by the sides and held him out, using his forefingers to lift Wilkin's arms so the dwarf resembled a highly distraught cross.

Alvisor courageously slipped behind Roger and pressed his back against the rear of the cave. Then the Magus pressed his own back against the rear of the cave. He and Roger were still hunkered on their knees.

"Would you like a lullaby?" Roger babbled.

The towering discarnate took one slow, sliding step toward the trio.

"Several lullabies?" Roger offered. His voice was so cracked from terror it should not have held together well enough for him to speak.

The specter took another slow, sliding step forward.

"Magic!" Wilkin screamed. "We're magic! The old,

pruned up, red-beard has magic! Let us zoom out of here! I won't warn you more than *six* additional times! Even a psychotic ghost can be hurt with magic!"

Zukove laughed, like a cross between a rabid gorilla and Satan's insane, mongrel brother, and took another slow, sliding step closer. The Wedsell dislodger levitated from the cave floor and into the misty, deformed hand.

Roger began waving Wilkin at the specter, trying to disorient the evil spook. "Alvisor!" he hissed. "Do something! You should be able to dredge up enough magic to save us from an immaterial entity!"

Alvisor's eyes were turned in opposite directions. His hands were flat atop his head and his beard was glowing blue and moving in the air like a drunken snake. He started mumbling. The words were unbelievable. Roger could not comprehend them. Wilkin's ears became pointed at them, and he began shaking harder.

The Wedsell dislodger unfolded and its pronged tip stopped just inches from Wilkin's wrinkled and sweat-soaked forehead.

Suddenly, Alvisor spoke loud and clear: "Walking backwards, but walking tall. Walking circles, or not at all. Walking backwards, down the hall. Don't walk forwards, it will make you squall!"

"Nooo!" Zukove screamed, sounding shamefully pitiful. "You heartless, filthy, disarmingly clever—" His words were choked off and he began swirling like a cloud in an atomic powered eggbeater.

Propelled by Alvisor's meager magic, the Wedsell dislodger flipped eerily around in the air. Its deadly tips, with dazzling swiftness, pared the specter into a thousand wisps. They swirled weirdly and chaotically until they vanished. The blade refolded and clattered to the stone floor.

Alvisor's beard ceased glowing and floating.

Roger crawled out of the cave. Alvisor was inert on the Earthman's back. Wilkin was attached to Roger's side like a second body. Under Roger's nose, burned into the dusty brown earth, and barely revealed by the weak, red light of the evening sun, was the vile gloved hand grasping the miserable, HackHell globe.

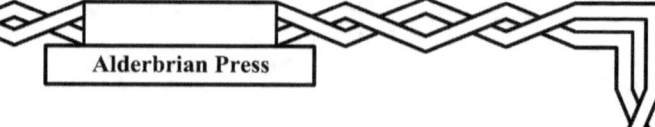
Chapter 13
Devil's Foot!

"We don't want to attract any attention while we're creeping through this fire bed," Alvisor said, with a cracking voice. "So walk softly and breathe as seldom as possible!"

It was gray evening. The crushed glass and mud brick walls of the town unmercifully chopped the road in half; a festering sore spot on the grassy landscape.

"What's the name of this place?" Wilkin said, with unbridled suspicion.

"They call it, Devil's Foot!" Alvisor admitted, with a white face.

"Devil's Foot!" Wilkin said, with a starkly horrified gasp. His tiny teeth chattered, sounding like a convention of drunken craps shooters. "Just as I feared! If I'd a known you'd even imagined going through here, I'd a stayed home drunk!"

"Is the town *that* bad?" Roger said, with a weak, high voice. His skin was tingling in apprehension.

"*Bad!*" Wilkin screamed. "What's the worst place you've ever been?"

"I was in a cage filled with preying mantises once," Roger confessed, with a blush, then a fine blanch. "That was bad!"

"Picture a hole five hundred times more terrible and subtract all the nice parts!" Wilkin said, squalling. "That's Devil's Foot!"

Roger felt so scared, he was sure his soul had fled his body.

Like repentant sinners approaching hell, the trio crept nearer to the huge, spear-tipped, iron gates of the vile city.

Even the architecture of the town is evil, Roger reflected. The buildings were composed of blood-red bricks, and festooned with steep spires and sharp corners. The glowering streets were hard-packed, black earth; bumpy and wide. For a fast getaway, he assumed.

From somewhere in the cancerous bowels of the city, there came several gunshots, then cruel, raucous laughter.

Roger began to shake like a sack full of fat dangling from the yardarm of a lurching schooner caught in the throes of an endless gale. Behind him, Wilkin was murmuring: "Oh, my glod! Oh, my glod! Oh, my glod!" Ahead of him, Alvisor appeared even more deathly pale. Which seemed impossible. Oh, lord! he thought. If the rest of the trip is like this, I'll never survive to get home. "Alvisor," he said, "is this animat-

ed graveyard really that bad?"

"Yeah," Alvisor comforted. "As far as I know, anybody decent who ever bungled in, ain't ever come out again!"

"Maybe they like it too much in there to leave," Roger raved, with heart-warming, child-like hopefulness.

"Ain't true!" Alvisor said. "Those noises should convince you of that!"

"Maybe the guard won't let us in?" Roger whispered.

"Use your stale-air-filled head," Alvisor said. "With this town's reputation, do you think they need a guard to keep people *out*? Most decent persons won't even propel diseased spit inside. The other kind will get in, sentry or not. And, as you can see for yourself, the gate's half open and untended."

"Yeah," Roger said. "Yeah."

"Now that we've got that to-do straight," Alvisor said, "lead the way, mister tough nuts, I want to return to my own damn world, wayfarer."

"*Me*!" Roger screamed, looking like a bull had chosen him for goring practice. "Why *me*? You're my guide! *You* should go first! Logic demands it!"

"I was afraid of that," Alvisor whined. "Damn logic! I'd like to slay whoever invented it!"

"You'd be a mass murderer," Roger said.

"Only if I took it into my scintillating mind to slay you!" Alvisor snapped.

"Oh, glod! Oh, glod!" Wilkin bawled. "We're gonna get butchered and all sorts of horrible things will happen to us, too!"

"Shut up!" Alvisor ordered. "I told you, we don't want to attract any attention! If one of those tough Hals in town sees you blubbering, we'll really be in the commode hole!"

"I'll try not to cry," Wilkin said, sobbing mournfully. He yanked a filthy handkerchief out of his right back pocket and dabbed at his soaking wet cheeks.

"Why don't you light up a cigarette?" Roger said. "That way, they'll figure you're a real tough Tom."

"You think so?" Wilkin said hopefully. He stuffed the handkerchief into his back pocket.

Roger would have burned the foul, tattered rag. "The only thing that would really help us, is a fully-automatic, army assault weapon," he muttered.

"I'll try a turkey fag anyway!" Wilkin stated. "At least it'll calm my nerves!"

"The only thing likely to calm your hair-trigger nerves, is a vicious blow to your over-ripe, melon-shaped head!" Alvisor said, with a growl.

"No need to get nasty and parental with him," Roger scolded.

"We're inside the gates!" Wilkin announced, with marvelment. "Now what?"

"We seek this hotel I know of," Alvisor said. "We'll be safer there than in any of the other vermin infested dives in town. We can order the stuff we need, through the staff. I know the manager—the mealy mouthed bastard! He owes me a favor for one I gifted him once near my tree. And it don't matter what kind, Wilkin! I might have a little trouble getting him to repay me, but that's to be expected in this odious, Wedsell skinning pit!"

"I hope it won't cost any of us an arm and or a leg," Roger said.

"Quiet now!" Alvisor warned darkly. "The fiends in this mortuary will cut you as soon as look at you! They'll even amputate your head because of the way you're *dressed*!"

Roger gaped at his P.J. top and the sea tossed shakes made friends with him again. He was also joined by a cold sweat.

They were passing along a dim side street. It was lined with bars which must have been designed by madmen without eyes. Some of the doors were upside down, and they opened from the bottom up, like reverse drawbridges. This seemed fine with the patrons, many of what were sprawled, drunk, in the doorways.

One of the quaint pubs boasted a revolving door painted to look like a guillotine. Several of what resembled men, were lounging against the red-brick front wall. They did not appear to be blood-vomiting drunk.

Roger thought they looked like Satan's favorite pupils. They wore thick funereal-black body stockings. Long, leather aprons, with numerous deep pockets, were hung from their bull necks and tied around their sinewy waists. Blood red boots completed their Gothic ensemble.

One of those glaring loiterers looked like a spastic knife thrower had repeatedly used his face for target practice. He was the most human appearing fiend in the group.

Roger hid beside Alvisor so the men would not note his infantile raiment and become psychotically incensed.

Three blocks down, Alvisor pointed to the hotel he wanted.

It was like all of Roger's nightmares involving mysterious threatening buildings in isolated, distorted locations. Six gigantic black cones were turned upside down on top of a three story high blue wedge. There were as many circular windows in the structure as there are holes in Swiss cheese, but only one door: a round hole seven feet in circumference.

Roger thought the lobby was almost nice. If wooden chairs, equipped with padded seat belts, and bolted into wooden pits in the rough, dirty, urine reeking floor, was your diseased idea of mondo pleasant.

The long brown registration counter was topped with a bed of needle sharp nails. An old quill pen stood in the ink pot which sat atop the open registry book.

The clerk's black braided hair was wound into a cone atop his head. His dismal pocked face was made for the torture pits in the deepest chasm of anybody's favorite, private hell. His upper front teeth were missing. He was gaily dressed in a blood red shirt and pants. A pistol and holster were strapped around his chest and left shoulder. "Three!" he stated, as though he would brook no disagreement. His voice sounded like bones being crunched. "Don't break the furniture and I won't have to shoot your tits off! Don't whine in the night if you get into trouble because you left your door unbolted! And, don't shit on the demon damned sheets!" He tossed a square key at Wilkin and glared at Roger as though he had abominated the Earthman all his unnatural life.

Roger ducked his head and reached for the quill pen.

"You're dead on slats if you do!" the piqued clerk said suggestively. "Nobody *ever* signs in! That way, we don't have to account for no body not coming back down!"

Wilkin sucked his thumb noisily for a couple of moments.

"I thought you said you knew this guy?" Roger said to Alvisor.

The clerk was staring holes in the Earthman. Unbelievably massive holes, according to the almost human expression smoldering in his psycho eyes.

"I did," Alvisor said, "but somebody cut off his extra two arms and he's apparently blocked past remem-beries from his crippled head, so he don't recall his good buddy. And, I suspect the guy who cut him, looked a lot like you."

"If we get to our room, real pronto," Roger whined, "maybe he'll forget I'm here."

The clerk drew his big pistol and fired seven times past Roger's right ear.

There was a scrabbling sound, produced by some-thing undeniably huge, and a new door was battered through the wall facing the street, before the trio could turn their quaking heads to stare in terror.

"*Damn rat!*" the clerk railed. "Eats half the living clientèle, if I don't keep it out of here! *Damn rat!*" He reached jerkily under the counter for a cardboard box and reloaded the pistol. Then, like a grisly ballet dancer, he leaped onto the nail-bed counter and laid down to rest, using the registry for a pillow. Roger was appar-ently of no further interest to his waffled mind.

It did not matter anyway. When the last shot had been fired, Alvisor had taken the key from down Wilk-in's pants and had fled up the nearest of six stairways. Roger and Wilkin were so close behind the fleeing ma-gician, they all looked like one fat man billowing up the stairs.

They traveled three circular flights of stairs, always going up, then ventured down a long, twisting hall-way. Their every apprehensive step was illuminated

by candle chandeliers shaped like brass knuckles. This section of the hotel was decorated like a vivisection laboratory. It was almost enough to make your heart pound its way out of your fear constricted chest.

Was this everything the cheery hotel had to offer? By no stretch of an insane asylum patient's delusion fraught imagination.

All along the hallway, many pairs of wild eyes surveyed the trio from numerous dark corners and ajar doors. They passed one wide open portal.

Roger tried meekly to peek inside.

A dark, hairy, bent-over form slammed the door shut.

Occasionally, a transom creaked open.

When Roger glanced fearfully up, each snapped closed.

Wilkin also noticed the attention they were receiving. He was gripping one of Roger's legs so tightly, it was becoming numb, heavy and nearly useless.

Roger pried Wilkin's mitts loose and swatted him on the side of the neck. "Take it easy," he soothed the dwarf. "We'll be in our room soon, son. We'll be sort of safe there."

"What if the owner of one of them pairs of spooky eyes jumps out with a knife and cuts our throats before we reach our hidey hole?" Wilkin said, pitiably.

"We won't have to pay the hotel bill," Roger said, ashamed by the lameness of his response.

They rounded a corner and froze in their reluctant tracks.

A tall, puce-robed stranger was standing at the door of the trio's intended sanctuary. He was fumbling with a ludicrously large ring of master keys. When he noticed the trio, he blushed, whirled around, and raced the opposite way down the dim hallway.

When the mysterious skulker's footsteps humanely faded to blessed silence, Alvisor nervously unlocked their door. They gasped with shock and disbelief!

Its candle chandelier illuminated, quite well, the daggers and other odd cutting tools sticking out of just about everything. Out of the chest of drawers to their left. Out of the two closet doors to their right. Out of the king sized bed against the wall facing them. Out of the three rickety chairs on their backs around the flimsy, knife-pierced table in the center of the room.

When Roger closed the door, twenty-five of the bodkins fell out of it. "This sure is a funny reception," he said, to no one in particular, seeing absolutely nothing funny about it.

"Never mind," Alvisor said. "Help me ditch these pimple poppers." He tiptoed alongside the bed to the one round window, flipped it open like a porthole, and began tossing the knives outside.

"Aren't you afraid somebody will get hurt?" Roger said. He followed the shaman's careless example.

Alvisor yanked a sword out of the head board of the

bed. "Hell, no," he grunted, "there's probably some foam-ing cur down there collecting them to sell to thieves and back-stabbers, otherwise known as politicians." He sent the sword outside as though it were a spear.

"You know anyone here who wants revenge on you, Alvisor?" Roger said. "The clerk's asleep, so this nostalgic welcome isn't for me." He caught a knife with the toe of his shoe, kicking the sticker neatly out the window.

"Naw," Alvisor said. "I've outlived all my born ene-mies. Except for Mavis Grunkel. But I don't think she leaves her lair any more, even to get at men. And, we all know, of course, Wilkin, there, is universally be-loved."

"Sweet, blinding truth," Wilkin said. "A rarity from your old, leathery lips." He handed the loose knives which had fallen from the hallway portal to Roger for proper, responsible disposal.

"Do you suppose The Monster orchestrated this homecoming gala?" Roger said.

"Naw," Alvisor said. "His style is like those bar suckers we saw. Expert knifers: Out of the dark, in a cowardly fashion, from behind, and slash! I reckon all this grief was for the previous occupant. The skink we interrupted probably installed them to scare the pre-vious occupant out and was about to retrieve his suc-cessful warning devices when we flew in."

"I hope he won't be mad 'cause we threw his gear

out, and do away with us during the thick of the night, to sell our bodies for unnatural and very disturbing purposes, to make up for his keen losses," Wilkin said. He tugged at a knife that was half as long as he was tall. It came free of the wall with a creaking sound, and he fell backwards. The knife flew from his hands, barely missing Alvisor's pointed nose, and stuck into the floor next to Roger.

"That was a neat trick," Roger said. He withdrew the blade and heaved it into the oblivious night. "Try it again, and we'll toss *you* out the window to the black market curs."

"What's the matter with your eyes?" Wilkin said. "It was a accident. If I'd a done it on purpose I wouldn't have missed! We Dwarfs are awful swift and handy with trimming utensils!"

"Especially in dark, damp places," Alvisor whispered to Roger. "Swish! One swipe and they can sever your shoe laces or cut holes in the knees of your pants!"

Roger chuckled, threw the last of the knives out the window, and closed that pneumonia hole. "I don't know about you Freds," he said, "but I'm hungry."

"So am I," Wilkin confessed, as if hunger were an unforgivable sin. "But I don't feel like sneaking down that hall to no eat-shack."

"All we gotta do is summon Room Service," Alvisor said. Next to the hall door, was a small wooden funnel, screwed to a square wooden box, bolted to the wall. He whistled piercingly into this advanced communications device. "What you guys want?" he said.

"We'll trust you to order," Roger said, words he feared he would probably live to regret. "But make it good. Preferably actually edible."

"Sure thing," Alvisor said. He pressed an ear to the funnel, then he shoved his mouth into it and spoke for what seemed like forever. "I took the liberty of ordering some first class booze," he told his weary pals.

"Fine," Roger said, "but I'm abstaining."

Alvisor winked condescendingly. "Whatever keeps you smiling," he said.

Wilkin righted and climbed into one of the weak chairs. He removed his boots, wiggled his pink toes and set the boots aside. "Why don't you make yourself comfortable, Roger, while you've got the chance?" he said.

Roger shook his head and wandered around the sham room, inspecting the pretend furnishings.

Alvisor visited the bed. Within seconds, he was loudly snoring.

Roger went to the shabby dresser and pulled out the top drawer. It was empty except for a slip of paper stuck to the bottom by a penknife. He jerked the paper loose and read its message softly aloud to himself: "In spite of everything, you're still brainlessly here. Too bad, you walking stink!" Rattled, he closed the drawer, crumpled up the note, and stuffed it into a crack in the wall by the door.

Though the note had not been from The Monster, perhaps, Roger still did not look into the other drawers; he was afraid he would find a crazy assassin, who was all too eager to pounce, scrunched into one of the bigger drawers.

A soft tapping startled him. When he recognized what the sound had been, he crawled from under the bed and reluctantly opened the door.

Someone had snuffed out half the candles in the hall chandeliers. Roger could barely see the uniformed figure and serving cart. As soon as the man and the conveyance were in the room, Roger closed and re-bolted the door.

The bellman straightened his Boy Scout uniform, checked the gun in the swivel holster strapped to his hip and looked at Roger with curiosity. "Your order, sir," he said, almost politely.

"Thank you," Roger said, almost politely. He dipped into Alvisor's money pouch and withdrew the smallest coin he could find.

Wilkin was asleep, hanging half out of his chair.

Roger could not ask the dwarf if the tip which he was about to bestow upon the snotty bellman was as insultingly small as he intended. He trusted to luck and handed the tiny coin over.

The bellman's face screwed up with an expression of utter revulsion.

This vindicated Roger's decision. He smiled, almost politely, and allowed the man to egress, bolting the door after him.

The acrid aroma of the food revived Wilkin and Alvisor. They dragged the three chairs up around the cart and seated themselves.

Alvisor took a gallon sized jug from the bottom shelf. He filled three crummy glasses with a pinkish liquid and set the jug on the floor next to him. "I poured it for you," he said, "but I ain't gonna lift it and drink it for you." He and Wilkin greedily held their glasses high.

Roger reluctantly did likewise.

Wilkin and Alvisor smacked their lips and whistled in appreciation of the liquor.

Roger wiped his bloodshot eyes and hoped the thirty alarm fire would soon die out. His anti-drinking conviction became stronger.

Alvisor and Wilkin refilled their glasses repeatedly. By the time the vegetable and banana dinner was over, they were well on their way to being dead drunk.

Roger watched them in silence and sighed. He could see he was not going to have a restful night. But he was determined to make the best of it. He gathered their plates, the jug, their licked dry glasses and the scattered silverware, off the floor and placed them all neatly on the cart the way his unusual mother use to lay fish heads out on the driveway.

Wilkin pointed at Roger and giggled, sounding like

marbles falling on aluminum foil stretched over a pot.

Alvisor nodded, causing him to pitch forward out of his chair. He struggled to his feet and unsteadily straightened his robe. "Let me take care of this bad ol' cart for you, Roger, ol' buddy," he slurred as he wheeled it up to the hall door. "Will you unlock the ol' portal fer me, hic! Rog–ger–ger–ger, ol' friend?" he said.

In resignation, Roger did as he was bid.

Alvisor staggered the cart into the hallway. After licking his forefinger and testing for wind in all four directions, he gave the cart a clumsy shove and watched it careen into the semi darkness.

There was an almost immediate ouch, then a loud crash.

Alvisor sniggered, reeled back into the room and closed the door by falling backwards against it.

"Why did you do that?" Roger demanded.

"Don' worry none," Alvisor slurred, "they'll fin' it inna mornin' an' take real good care of it."

"Yeah, but you hit somebody!" Roger scolded.

"So wh–what?" Alvisor said, belligerently.

Roger sadly realized rational discourse would be futile. He said nothing, thought even less and bolted the door.

Alvisor began wandering drunkenly around the sham room and peering at the ceiling.

Wilkin rocked back and forth in his chair, shaking with laughter. "That sure was funny, Al," he said, with a gasp. "Got ol' Roger all 'cited an' 'cerned! Gasp! Ya know any good songs?"

"It would cost me my life!" Alvisor shouted, cackling like a squadron of excited geese.

"Was a lot of socks," Wilkin slurped suddenly. "Soggy socks, all sewn together into a fab bedspread. Used it like a tornado to pick all my paw's potatoes. But slipped back into the lapo of luxury and gagged." He sucked in a deep breath to rave further, but fell asleep on his chair, with his mouth open wide.

Alvisor's eyes grew glassy. He passed out and slumped to the floor.

Roger sat down on the bed and tried to concentrate. Maybe he could duplicate the ugly conditions which precipitated his popping into—Snooglela—and zap himself back to his apartment.

After all, Alvisor could be wrong about his spell and the lightnings. They may have had no part in his translation to Snooglela. It might have just been his following of the instructions in the self-improvement book. The idea was worth a try, at the least, most, best and worst.

"First," Roger said, in a monotone with which he intended to mesmerize himself, "he must enjoy a satisfying meal." He had, he guessed. "Second, he should be completely alone." With all-knowing Alvisor and fearless Wilkin passed out, it's like being secluded, he thought. "Third, he must be in as perfect a state of silence as possible."

Alvisor and Wilkin were barely breathing at the moment, so it was comfortingly quiet.

Roger smiled hopefully. That funny feeling was in his stomach, like when he entered lovely, heart warming Snooglela. He just hoped it wasn't the odd meal or the booze he ingested.

"The subject must make himself as comfortable as possible, preferably in a supine position," Roger continued, still performing a beautiful job of monotoning.

When he tried to lie down, he was surprised to find himself already flat on his back on the bed. It's working, he thought, groggily. In five meager minutes, home!

He strained to remember the rest of the instructions. He was so sleepy from the combination of exhaustion, food and booze, he could only paraphrase:

"Close eyes, take deep breath, continuously mentally repeat first name backwards."

His deep, loud, rude, breath turned into an even deeper, louder, ruder yawn. "Jus' like las' time," he said sluggishly. Regor, Regor, Regor, he thought eagerly.

Then he plummeted into sleep.

***

A fire alarm howled raggedly.

Roger found himself seated behind his shabby desk in Zolo's Accounting Firm. Across from him, the door to the Manager's Office was wide open. Thick smoke was pouring out, and a greenish fire was consuming the manager's expansive desk. A threatening, black-habited figure stood fanning the flames, using its huge, gloved hands.

All around Roger, his co-workers were fleeing the fiery threat. Some were riding on wheeled tables and chairs through gaping doorways. Others were leaping out windows. He watched the last of his cowardly co-workers vanish, then observed the flames advancing toward the Manager's doorway.

Fleeing for his disappointing life would be useless, so he took a deep breath of the smoggy air breezing in through the closed bay window behind him and opened his five desk drawers. Carefully, he dumped their contents onto the floor, into a messy pile. He flipped the drawers upside down and stacked them on top of one another on the surface of the crappy desk.

The figure in the black habit tossed a bucketful of gasoline onto the fire and there was an explosion in the Manager's Office. The flames flared out into Roger's desk space. He stood up in his worn chair and stepped onto the highest drawer.

There was another explosion and the green fire encircled his desk. The flames finally got to the sprinklers and they came on full, flooding him with cold water. He gasped for air and held his arms toward the ceiling. But there was no way out for him there!

***

Roger awoke with a mighty startlement. His clever

teleportation attempt had failed dismally. He felt no disappointment from this. Probably because his brain and body were weirdly numb from his sleeping head down in a large wastepaper basket. The glass of booze he swilled had landed him a delayed clobber which had rolled him off the bed and into the trash. He extricated himself from the basket and began pinching his jerky, misbehaving body back to a semblance of normal circulation.

Alvisor was sprawled on his gut on an ironing board he had discovered in the closet. He had planned to use the board as a mighty tongue depressor to examine the dwarf's amazing mouth. Mercifully, unconsciousness had intervened, again.

Wilkin was asleep atop an upside down flat iron. He had one of his big toes stuck into one of his small ears.

Roger sighed. He was really still half asleep and partially numb. He plopped face down on the bed. "So much for single valiant efforts to return home," he mumbled.

Chapter 14
Roger Dodger

Morning arrived with a dull thud and a loud groan in the hallway, jolting Roger from uncomfortable sleep. He crawled from between the worn mattress and the wooden support slats, sat down on the bed, and peered groggily around the room.

Alvisor was standing on his head in the corner to the right of the hall door. His beard was curled around his ankles, keeping his robe from dropping. His mustache covered his eyes and there was a strange smile on his face. A shaft of sunlight through the round window made him appear more surreal than ever.

Wilkin had rolled off the flat iron, into the waste basket, getting lodged crosswise.

Roger had never seen an iron so huge. It looked half as large as the king sized bed. Drunken Wilkin had mistaken it for the bed. Roger marveled at Alvisor's ability to even lift the flat iron, let alone carry it out of the closet and across the room.

Roger slid off the creaky bed and weaved into the bathroom. He had assumed it was just another closet and would have kept said assumption if Alvisor or Wilkin had not opened its heavy door at some mysterious time during the equally mystifying night.

When Roger exited the stinky W.C., he noted Alvisor had modified his position. The old man's left leg was bent backwards and his left foot was tucked behind his right ear. Roger stopped rubbing his amazed eyes and gave the waste basket a kick.

It flipped over hard and Wilkin tumbled out, as limp as a cheap rubber spider. He rolled grotesquely until he flopped against the wall to the left of the hallway door. After various strange and terrible contortions, he arose and stared reproachfully at Roger. "Kick a man when he's down and asleep, huh?" he said. "Fun and laughs, huh? Watch the little man roll like a hairy ball, huh? Well, I'm gonna get even with you some how —if my hangover ever goes away!" He pressed his hands against the sides of his head and moaned. Then he leaned forward and peered hard. "My feet!" he quavered. "My snot damned, precious feet!"

"What about your foul feet?" Roger asked, with intense and undisguised disinterest.

"They's both the same size!" Wilkin screamed. He covered his tragic eyes with his tiny, horrified hands. "The *same* damned *size!*"

"Still drunk," Roger mumbled, with disgust. He limply sat down on the bed. "Probably be drunk for sixty years. Swilled enough. Drank a Nile River full. Downed an ocean. Started to squirt out of their ears and nostrils. Got the walls wet. Killed the sad roaches who asked only for a quiet life. Shamed my parents. And whistled religious music all night in their sleep. Damned queer. The people on this planet, are damned queer."

A sudden crash rattled the window. Alvisor had fallen out of the corner. He was now draped over the waste basket. He continued to flash his strange smile.

Roger helped Wilkin roll Alvisor off the waste basket and onto his back. Roger rolled Alvisor off Wilkin's back, then onto his own back. Wilkin rolled Alvisor off Roger's back and they both disgustedly rolled Alvisor, finally, onto the Magus's back.

Alvisor's beard shot straight up, then it collapsed into a coil on his chest. His eyes flew open and he got unsteadily to his feet.

"Let's go find some breakfast," Roger said.

Alvisor and Wilkin hunched over, making retching sounds.

"Sorry," Roger said, trying not to laugh. "Did you get your feet squared away, Wilkin?"

"Yeah," Wilkin bubbled. "Was my eyes. The spaz-juice made one of them longer than it should a been and I saw evenness on my feet where it was absent before!"

That was the last straw! The horrible town, the horrible hotel, the horrible clerk and the idiot answer were too much for Roger to withstand stoically. He almost howled in misery. "Let's space-cadet out of here," he said instead, half out of the room, and his mind.

Wilkin leaped into his boots and clung to Alvisor who clung to Roger. They were in fear for their lives. An axe was cleaved into the top half of the outside of their door, and several daggers, artistically spelling the word DEATH, were stuck into the bottom half.

As the trio flew around the left corner, a door snapped open, banging against the wall like a fully laden semi tractor trailer spearing into a concrete bridge abutment at full throttle. Several knives twanged into the red-stained floor just behind them. The trio ran. They paid their hotel bill on the run.

When they were adjacent the already crowded bars, Alvisor stopped their wild flight. "There's a restaurant, past the square, toward the rear gates, I've heard of," he said. "We'll stop there, on the way out!"

An outbreak of violence transferred itself from one of the worst bars infesting Devil's Foot and into the weed covered square.

Roger and company stood at the edge of the huge square and watched the proceedings.

The center of the commotion was a man in baggy purple coveralls. His bulldog face appeared livid with rage, and he was rudely as large as a gorilla with a super hyper thyroid problem.

Gray clouds on upper strata winds blocked the sun from the square. Roger noticed this and felt inexplicably nervous.

"It appears we've lost our shortcut," Alvisor said. "We'll have to take the long way around."

"That might be best, genius" Roger said. "We'd be bound to be noticed nonchalantly crossing the square in the middle of a gut-wrenching fight to the death."

"No freaking kidding!" Wilkin piped.

A noisy crowd was swiftly gathering to join into the potential free for all.

As the adventurers crept through the mob, they kept their eyes on the center of the square.

The big man was facing an obviously brain dead man less than half his size. Shortie resembled a human rat in a black habit. The big man paid no attention to the throng. Shortie, however, was scrutinizing it.

Roger assumed Shortie was desperately seeking an escape opening in the tightly packed mob. "Hope the jerky little feller doesn't get horribly harmed," he muttered. "Sure wouldn't want to tangle with such a beast unless I had a hydrogen bomb with me." He came to an abrupt halt against Alvisor's back.

Wilkin bumped into Roger's posterior.

"What's the matter?" Roger said irritably.

"That ain't a real fight," Alvisor said, "it's just a put on to draw a crowd. That's The Monster's driver trying to sic that leviathan abuser of mountain ranges on *us!*"

Roger stared harder at Shortie. "You're right!" he said, with fearful recognition. "Let's fade out of here before he sights us!"

"It's too late!" Alvisor wailed. "We're in a spot where there's just the three of us!"

"Why the steaming, buttered-hell did you stop, then?" Roger demanded.

"Because I'm scared witless!" Alvisor screeched.

"You were *born* witless!" Wilkin shouted angrily.

"Go stick your head up your—"

"Let's flee, fools." Roger pleaded.

"We can't," Alvisor mourned. "The crowd won't allow it. Everyone's noticed the shitty driver fingering us. These people came for sordid excitement. They've circled us in to be sure king bruiser reaches us!"

"Look!" Wilkin said hoarsely.

Roger and Alvisor turned their heads.

The driver was pointing at them with both trembling hands and, true to his rodent like physiognomy, was falsely ratting on them; striving intensely to direct the creature's one track mind from himself, to them.

Roger assumed the vile rat-man was prevaricating slurs the trio supposedly had spoken about the horrid drooling ogre, or his shambling Neanderthal father, or his reeking Primate mother, or all of the afore mentioned.

The driver gestured weirdly several times while speaking in a swift, feverish way.

The bigger beast snorted like an irate bull and glared at Roger and company.

Following what was, no doubt, more nefarious lies, plus evil, spine-chilling suggestions of how the hirsute thug could exact revenge upon Roger and company, the driver scuttled into the safety of the crowd.

The wild eyed bruiser lumbered toward the hapless trio.

***

Behind the rowdy crowd, the intimidating coach waited at a corner of the square. The left curtain was rolled up and The Monster's threatening form could barely be discerned in the inner darkness.

The driver exited the mob in haste. He was wiping his sweat soaked brow with the sleeve of his grimy habit. He climbed into his seat. "I have deceived Norgrum at them, now, master. Norgrum is good at his reprehensible work!"

"You avoided paying the slayer?" The Monster said, with surprise.

"Yes, master! Forgive me, master!"

"An amazing and vastly puzzling glimmer of intellect," The Monster marveled. "For that, you may keep the slayer's fee."

"Thank you, master! Bless you, master! You are much too beneficent, royal master!"

"Over sniveling may cost you the riches you have just, no doubt, accidentally gained," The Monster warned.

"Forgive me, master!" the driver said, with fervor. He greedily fingered the pouch of glod that hung with such delightful heaviness in the right pocket of his habit.

"Only Aleron can save them from Norgrum," The Monster said, gloating with record setting intensity. "I doubt that vaunted, goody-beans sorcerer is still able to cast spit due to my ingenious Obstruction Spell, or he would already have intervened on behalf of those chaotically hopping, bulge-eyed insects."

"Shall we press on, master? Or can we watch?" the driver begged. He enjoyed observing a good assassination as much as the next gibbering ghoul.

"On!" The Monster ordered. "Soon, the only obstacle between myself and Aleron will be delightfully short distance!"

***

Roger took a quick gape left and right at the constituents of the lynch mob. It was obvious they were members in good standing of The Cruelty Club of The Universe. He hoped his death would be swift. He knew it wouldn't be painless.

Wilkin crouched and covered his head with his arms.

Alvisor looked as though he were trying to disappear.

Like an elephant about to trunk-whack a clueless duck, the ugly bruiser loomed over Roger. He glowered and curled his upper lip. "I'm called Norgrum," he rumbled, like an overloaded truck in low gear on a steep incline, "and I'm gonna separate your blubbery body from your insignificant soul!"

Face to navel with Norgrum, Roger heard Alvisor muttering some witless phrases. The old fart's gone ploosey on me, he thought. I hope Wilkin finds a sunny burial plot for my greasy shards. A thunderous snarl shook him back to tasteless reality.

"I said, fight, you grotesque, yellow livered, ball of stinking, fat!" Norgrum roared. He produced a nine fingered glove from his breast pocket and smacked Roger on the cheeks several times. Then he smacked the stiff glove multiple times against Roger's face.

True to his form, Roger turned and peered at his friends.

Wilkin was in a pile on the weeds. He was singing to his little knees.

Alvisor was standing beside the dwarf. The mighty magician was waving his arms and beard about, giving the impression he was suffering an unbelievably gross seizure.

Norgrum tossed the glove into the crowd, grabbed Roger painfully by one shoulder and whirled him around. He clamped hold of Roger's nose. "Are you gonna fight, to back up your ugly face and revolting words, or ain't you, you soft, green, slimy, smelly, bowel-baby!" he screamed in insulted rage.

In spite of his pain, Roger gained control of his right

hand and unbuttoned his pajama breast pocket. He withdrew his pocket watch and dangled it in front of Norgrum's bloated face. "Would the raging retard like a nice watch?" he said, with a gasp of desperation. "It keeps shockingly good time!"

Norgrum released Roger's nose. He swiped the watch and bit it in two. He bounced one half off Roger's forehead and spat out the remaining crunched glass, mangled gears, and gnawed case at Roger's feet. He started pounding on Roger's head. "Fight, damn you!" he demanded. "Rotten apples got more fight than you!"

Roger attempted to duck the eerily bouncing fist blows. He also made several feeble jabs at Norgrum but hit only thin air and hot crowd farts. The huge fist continued to rebound off the top of his stinging, ringing head. His eyes crossed and uncrossed, then the lids fluttered.

Alvisor was still issuing his witless ravings.

Wilkin had willed himself unconscious.

Small comfort for Roger, indeed.

Norgrum whirled Roger around and began kicking his fundament. His tiny pseudo-brain became unconfused and he began kicking Roger's flabby fundament instead.

Laughing with the leering, hooting crowd of Lucifer's Concerned Friends, Norgrum kicked Roger into an undignified heap, yanked him up by the back of his neck and kicked him down harder.

When Norgrum did not re-boot Roger off the weeds, he hoped the beast had gotten his thrills and slavered back to a bar, or the rusty cage from which he must have been released by the rat-man. He struggled to his feet and focused his eyes. Instead of relief flooding over him, his brain popped back and forth inside his throbbing skull.

Norgrum reached into a pocket of his overalls and pulled out a three foot long potato peeler!

Some helpful citizen tossed a long steel rod, with a thick wooden handle, at Norgrum's leviathan feet.

With his heart pounding out a frenzied lament, Roger realized this simple device could be only one thing. A skewer. Just for him! Norgrum was planning to skewer him and peel him like a helpless potato! "My mama scolded me repeatedly to stay in my little sand box!" he screamed, in dissociation. "I should have listened to that carping, harpy, bitch!"

Norgrum liked Roger's terror. He smiled and started toward Roger with the skewer held like the sword used to kill the tortured animal in a fair, brave and noble bull fight.

Fortune, however, rushed to Roger's assistance. Another of Alvisor's half remembered spells worked handsomely! More or less. Rather less, than more, actually.

Norgrum was suddenly faced with one hundred and twenty-five smirking Roger Lincolns. They joined hands and proceeded to dance a wild Mazurka around the slayer. He dropped his tools and whirled and whirled, like a marionette on a single string, as he tried to pick out the real Roger. Whenever he grabbed at one, his hairy hands passed through and the fake Roger wiggled in a masterfully lewd manner.

Roger was so relieved, he nearly giggled. He turned his back on the circus of illusions, sighted the top of Alvisor's head, and wended his way through the chortling crowd. It was obvious the malevolent Mergatroids did not see him.

Alvisor was holding unconscious Wilkin by one arm. He smiled and shrugged.

Roger smiled back, then grabbed Wilkin by the seat of the pants and helped Alvisor carry him.

They ran along a street lined by scary looking whore houses and terrifying bars, turning down the first filthy alley they chanced upon. They made half a dozen more such aimless course changes before they halted at the back of a sad and sticky looking restaurant.

Roger and Alvisor dropped Wilkin flat on his back on the cobblestone walkway. They proceeded to slap the dwarf back to consciousness.

"What happened?" Roger asked. He gave Wilkin a solid whack on the chest.

"Search me," Alvisor said. He kicked the dwarf on one hip. "When I saw you was in dire jeopardy, all I knowed was I had to help my great friend in some way not requiring me to leave my own head behind on the urine soaked square."

"You went about it with considerable strangeness, but, thanks, anyway," Roger said. He jabbed Wilkin in the kidneys.

"Think almost nothing of it," Alvisor said. He twisted Wilkin's left ear and slapped him across his big mouth. He gave Roger an apologetic look for having missed his mark, then slapped Wilkin across the mouth. "I was surprised at the form my Trouble Extraction Spell took, too. It was supposed to fly us sixty feet away from the crowd for the desperate running room we required!"

"How long do you think it's gonna take to wake him up?" Roger said. He knocked on the top of the dwarf's head like it was somebody's front door and he was checking to see if anyone was home.

"Dunno," Alvisor judged. "Could take—He's coming out of it now." He delivered Wilkin a final hard rap on his chest and they both stood back.

Wilkin's eyes snapped open and he gaped at Roger's many bruises, cuts and abrasions. "Uncle Twiddley's returned from the grave!" he screamed. "Don't take me, Uncle Twiddley! I *tried* to be holy! I always burned a Wedsell on Uncle's Day! And I never took more'en *five* swaks of glod at any one time!"

Roger jerked the dwarf into a sitting position. "I'm not your Uncle Twiddley," he said, through clenched teeth, "I'm poor, sinned against *Roger*."

Wilkin rubbed his bugged out eyes. He peered and

peered at Roger. "You're right," he finally said, with humiliating relief. "You're not my Uncle Twiddley. My Uncle Twiddley was much *finer* looking!"

"Thanks a *lot*," Roger said.

"How'd we escape and get here?" Wilkin asked.

"Alvisor got jiggy with magic and created phantoms of me to distract Norgrum and the crowd while we hauled your lazy, sleeping ass to safety," Roger said.

"Wasn't being lazy or sleeping," Wilkin lied, "was playing dead, waiting for my chance to strike in your defense."

"You sure fooled us," Alvisor said, with notable sarcasm. "Poor Norgrum's lucky you didn't have a chance to attack."

"Aww, go guzzle puke," Wilkin said, trying not to look embarrassed.

"By the by," Roger said, "how long will those copies of my winsome self be high kicking around?"

Alvisor wound his beard tips around one of his ears in a obvious and pitiable effort to think. "About an hour, I guess," he said.

"That'll allow us time to get something to eat," Roger said. "Before we flee this children's vacation paradise."

Wilkin considered the rear door of the restaurant. His eyes shone with excitement and his tongue fell out of his trembling mouth.

Alvisor stiffened. "I'll fetch the food!" he said, hastily. "You two wait here!"

"I want—"

"Whatever I get, short shafts!" Alvisor snapped. He lurched through the filthy door. He was outside again almost as quickly as he had entered. He handed out paper sacks filled with what was probably some type of deep-fat fried fruit.

Before Roger had finished his food, his sack was soggy with tears.

Wilkin's face was slightly green.

Alvisor, however, was smiling. He was satisfied with the meal as well as the price; nothing! The stuff was at least a day old. He did not tell his friends this. He was afraid they would make him go back in for more. He had embarrassed himself too much while begging and bawling for the first handout to go through that entire self-effacing routine again. Even he had his limits, incredibly low though they were.

Wilkin regained his natural color. He began puffing on a cigarette.

Roger stemmed his flow of tears. "We've got to scatter dust," he said. "We don't want to remain in town after those illusions of my manly self sadly fade away."

"Yes sir, boss man, chief, captain and what not," Wilkin said. He took a final drag on his root beer flavored cigarette and tossed his butt at an inebriated roach staggering along the wall of the restaurant. Then he threw the fag butt at the insect. He missed with both shots.

The roach swaggered away.

"Lead the way, Alvisor," Roger said.

"Righto!"

The rest of the alley was bordered by stables and Horse Sales Offices. On their way through the gaping rear gates, the fortunate trio latched onto three horses equipped with full saddles and tack.

Alvisor kissed his still greasy fingertips. "Spell worked!" he said happily. "Another of my patented conjurations functioned, just glossy fine! But," he confided, soberly, to Roger, "I just don't know what benefit I could have been to you, if The Monster's enlisted killer hadn't been the Town Sissy!"

Chapter 15

Mavis's Girdle

The wide road from Devil's Foot looked like a dirty brown, slithering snake. Great chunks of gray rock glowered on the left. Trees and fields of brown grass stood beyond and between them. Great chunks of gray rock loomed on the right, with the ominous, scorching, amber desert stretching beyond.

Roger and company rode their horses at a comfortable walk down the fat spine of the serpent. Alvisor was in the lead. Roger came next. Wilkin brought up the rear. Seems logical.

Devil's Foot was already out of sight.

Roger relaxed and settled into his saddle. The peaceful surroundings made him feel calm and benign. He could almost forget the events of the previous days. To even think of recalling them made him shiver and perspire.

Still, when he looked at his companions, his situation didn't seem so awful. In fact, knowing them was what made this nutso world feel bearable. And this was so, even though they had led him into the past series of life threatening escapades, and frantic, hair-narrow escapes.

There was one aspect which made up for all of this. It canceled out the somberness of the gray clouds obscuring the hot sun, and nearly made him forget about The Monster.

These men were his only real friends. His first pals.

On Earth, everyone was always after something. They were either so aggressive, pushy or thoughtless, they were cruel. Alvisor and Wilkin were not carbon copies of these people. They had done nothing but help him since his arrival on HackHell. That almost never happened on Earth, anymore.

The fluttering of a flock of yellow birds broke into his musings. He watched them soar overhead. He smiled. Such occurrences were becoming rare on Earth because air pollution made it nearly impossible to see above the tops of the sooty skyscrapers.

He groaned and reined his horse alongside Alvisor's. "Hey, aged man," he said. "We didn't stock up on any food in Devil's Foot."

Alvisor appeared embarrassed and unhappy. "I just realized that, too," he said.

"What'll we do?" Roger said. "We can't go back into Devil's Foot! Not even *God* can make me dip my toe twice into *that* seething acid bath!"

"Well, sir," Alvisor said. "Them is Sweet and Nut

Weeds around them boulders. Their tangled roots are edible and full of flavor and energy. It wouldn't take me half an hour to gather enough of those to last the rest of the trip. You get a fire going to roast them on. That brings out their best taste, and detoxifies them better than vinegar boiling, or repeated, sustained regurgitation. There's a nice spot." He pointed to a large slab of gray rock about fifty yards from the road. A clump of trees with round leaves provided cool shade for the long grass carpeting the area.

Roger barely paid attention, he was trying to grapple with Alvisor's words concerning the culinary preparation of the weeds. Repeated, sustained regurgitation? He shivered and abandoned his efforts for the sake of his remaining sanity. He and Alvisor reined in at the side of the road.

Wilkin evened up with them. "What's going on?" he asked. "You look like mighty generals plotting the capture of a sissy boy's prissy bathroom."

"Just talking about stopping so Alvisor can gather roots for us to—ugh—eat," Roger said. "He forgot to buy supplies in Devil's Foot."

"It figures he'd forget," Wilkin said. "It involves spending glod. But roots is the best idea *I've* had all day!"

Alvisor ambled his noble steed past the clump of trees and into taller grass.

Wilkin dismounted.

Roger followed suit and began gathering sticks and leaves.

Reluctantly, Wilkin pitched in.

Roger jerked the dwarf out of the few sticks already piled up and shook that scamp upside down for a while as a lesson to him.

After that, they worked in silence, going far and wide. Soon, they had a good-sized pile of brush. More like emergency bonfire size.

"I wonder where he is?" Wilkin muttered. "How long does it take to suck up weeds?"

Suck up weeds? Roger thought. He started to ask if Wilkin was speaking literally, but decided he really did not want an answer. "Alvisor said thirty minutes," he quietly replied. He was rubbing two sticks together above the brush. "You should know such things, you live on this world."

"We Forest Dwarfs buy everything we eat," Wilkin said, very snootily. "And it's been thirty minutes already."

"Let's give the old man another five," Roger decided. He threw the sticks down in disgust. "Hope he's got —" He fixed Wilkin with a look potent enough to rust wallpaper. "You've got those damned matches in your scummy pocket, yet you let me rub those sticks together, like some kind of an expert fool! You make sure this fire gets going when we need it, or even Satan will bawl his evil eyes bloody at what I'll do to you!"

"Ice out, Earthman," Wilkin said, in his own defense, "I thought you was exercising or practicing uncanny and scary religious rituals. I'm as ignorant about your customs as you are about mine."

"No matter how pretty it's packaged, it's still a reeking, jiggling load of maggot-ridden, bullshit," Roger enlightened the smirking dwarf.

***

The Five Minutes flew by quickly, then it returned and squatted in front of Roger and Wilkin, preening its, square, orange feathers.

Wilkin looked at Roger from the corners of his eyes.

Roger returned the glassy eyed look. "Let's allot him another couple of minutes," he uttered, with brave decision.

"And two hours," Wilkin mumbled. "And six weeks. And nine years. And all my snot damned life!" he yelled, muffling his words with his hands.

***

Morning became noon.

The Five Minutes flew off. It was tired of being improperly fondled by Wilkin.

Roger stretched lazily. "I guess we probably should go and see if he's all right," he said reluctantly. "He might have fallen asleep, popped out of his saddle, and busted his rough old face."

"I guess so," Wilkin said, with sarcasm and impatience.

"Do you know anything about tracking?" Roger said. He swung his sore fanny awkwardly into his saddle.

"I've never gone hunting in my superlative, roll-model life," Wilkin said proudly.

"Neither have I," Roger confessed. "Guess we'll have to hope he left a noticeable trail of death and or destruction in his wake."

"Don't train your ducks on it," Wilkin enthused. He gasped with surprise and dug his fingers into one of Roger's chubby calves. "Speaking of crazy," he whispered, "did you just see a pair of sickly eyes in that wall of rock, to our right?"

They were clopping along the road beside one of the huge gray chunks of stone, intending to veer left into the towering grass, where Alvisor had mysteriously vanished.

Roger peered hard at the dwarf. It hurt his pupils. "You're putting me on," he said. "Everybody knows rocks don't possess eyeballs."

"You better share your awesome, infallible, arcane wisdom with that rock!" Wilkin whispered. "I just saw its peepers again!"

Roger reined in his horse and whirled his head around. He stared at the towering rock, but saw nothing out of the ordinary. "You'd better not breathe through your mouth any more," he admonished, "the surplus oxygen is affecting your feeble mind."

A wide crack appeared in the rock and a large ugly shape sprang forth like a swollen tongue falling out of the mouth of a dead fish.

Wilkin screamed and fainted, propped against his horse's neck.

Roger grabbed Wilkin's reins and tried to heel his own steed into motion down the road.

The apparition lassoed the men and yanked them to the grass. Grunting and groaning, the captor dragged them into the huge rock and the crack snapped shut, like a politician's hands catching hold of taxpayer money.

The woman, for this is what their captor was, hauled the helpless, semiconscious men slowly down a long, narrow hallway hewn out of phosphorescent stone, and into a small cell. She removed the lasso and spasmodically kicked the prisoners until they regained consciousness.

Roger's first impression of the woman boggled his mind. She resembled an eighty year old prizefighter with dank, shoulder-length black hair, a bulbous nose, and piss-colored eyes. She was wearing coveralls decorated with big, pink polka dots.

Wilkin shot the bag a gape and tried to burrow into the shining stone floor.

The woman cackled. She slapped Wilkin to get his attention and oddly rocked side to side. "Pleased to meet you, studs," she croaked. "Don't get much company around here; only what's extremely weak in what's left of their minds. The name's Mavis. What's yours?"

Roger thought the woman's cognomen sounded familiar. He tried out his tongue, found it functioned reasonably well, and whispered his name.

"Roger, hey!" Mavis shrieked. "Don't like that shitty moniker! Don't like you either, blubber butt boy!" She grabbed a handful of Roger's gut. "Where's Al? I was promised he'd be with you? The leathery bastard sidewinder!" She reluctantly released her handful of flab.

Roger rubbed his injured area. "He got lost," he said sullenly.

"That's him," she said. "He'd get lost in his crusty shorts. No matter. He'll remember where he is and stumble-bum in here looking for you. I'll pounce on his skinny ass then. He's too old to recall enough spells to fool *me*. What's the little guys pringle?"

"Wilkin," Roger spat, through clenched teeth.

She studied Wilkin, much like a famished hawk ponders a sparrow. "He's kinda cute," she said. "I'm real fond of *him*!" She snatched hold of the horrified dwarf's arm and yanked him to his feet. "You'll do, honey," she cooed hoarsely. "Just what I'm aching for. Come with me!" She started dragging Wilkin toward the door.

Wilkin pleaded with Roger with his pitiful, little dwarf eyes.

Mavis spoke ominously over her pointed shoulder:

"Don't try to help your silky, shiny, pewee pal. I'm *very* good at magic. You wouldn't want to be an overripe, pink-winged, pond-scum-licking, singing turd, would you?"

The metal door slammed itself shut, with a heart breaking clang, and Roger was left in lonely semi-darkness. He fell, forlorn, on his back on the single, filthy bunk. He closed his eyes to concentrate on escape. But it was a futile effort. The mattress was lumpy, and several spectacled, lavender cockroaches decided to go mountain climbing on his stomach. He groaned, arose, and started pacing.

***

Roger grew tired of pacing and laid down on the bunk. The delegation of determined roaches again began their ascent to the summit of his stomach. He bellowed, jumped up, and ran to the imprisoning door.

Standing tip toe, he peered out its barred window. The dim hall was as empty, as he had expected, and as he had feared. He moaned and returned to the bunk.

If that brainiac Alvisor just hadn't gotten lost, he thought, we wouldn't have blundered into Mavis's trap.

Though he tried mightily not to, he could not keep from wondering what the witch was doing to Wilkin. He was probably a toad by now, hopping around in a fish bowl, and snapping flies out of the air with his long, red, sticky tongue.

This thought was too much for Roger. He yelled like

a timid, falsetto savage, leaped off the reeking bunk, and kicked with all his might. To his amazement and fear, the door shot off its thick hinges with a frightful sound of snapping metal, and skidded up against the hall wall with a resounding boom!

When he was not beaten to death by howling monsters or, worse, the sweaty witch, he moved his arms from around his head and stood up out of the corner to the left of the doorway.

He peeked up and down the hall, then shakily crept along it the way the witch had taken tragic, squalling, Wilkin. Probably to his doom. Wilkin Soup, or Little Dwarf Cookies.

Roger caught his stomach in an effort to heave bile and forced it, and his fevered imagination, to calm down.

He found another long corridor and was surprised to see it was illuminated by a single light bulb. When he came underneath the light, he saw it was actually a light-bulb-shaped container filled with some kind of bubbling, glowing chemical.

He traveled nervously until he came to a wooden door with a grilled window. He twisted the metal knob, but no luck. He stood on tip toe and peered through the grill. All he saw was a very coarse darkness. It was a cinch he would not venture into *that* room even if the door had not been locked!

He backtracked until he discovered a dim corridor

he had missed before. A bright glow outlined the doorway at the end, and a few unfamiliar sounds carried themselves to his unreceptive and apprehensive ears.

When he reached the bright light, he flattened himself against a wall and tried to peek inside.

There was one fine stench issuing from the great room. He thought it smelled like the Executive Washroom at the firm. But he could not be sure; his boss took his key away after he used it just once.

He decided to edge closer, for a better look, but his reluctant feet got tangled, and he fell on his nose. When he turned over, he was gazing into the cruel, green eyes of his unregenerate captor.

Mavis helped Roger to stand up. She used a very painful ear hold. "Took you long enough, honey," she said. "What happen, you forget how to open a door?"

Roger pulled his ear free. "Where's poor Wilkin?" he almost demanded. "What ugly crimes have you enacted upon his innocent and slightly perverted person?" He followed her point and gasped. "Wilkin!" he said. "You put your clothes back on, this minute! Do you hear me? Who do you think you are, running around all naked like that?"

Wilkin watered around the eyes. "She said she'd turn me into a ball of flea shit 'less I stripped!" he wailed.

"You betcha, sweet orbs," Mavis said. "I'm doing a

painting of him. Real fetching, too. Come look at it."

Roger had not noticed the old hag had moved. She was standing at an easel and was dabbing a paint brush at a large canvas.

The room was bare-walled rock. Besides the easel and canvas, and the brush and mixing board in Mavis's grimy hands, there was a small, oval, cluttered table to furnish it. The ceiling was glowing white; the sole source of the bright light. Probably more phosphorescence.

Roger stood aft the old lady and it was one macabre painting he unwillingly glommered! She had brushed in a lurid purple, velvet-textured, background, and it appeared Wilkin was cavorting with eight nude handmaidens, all of whom were the spitting image of the witch.

Roger suppressed a gag, feeling it would be notably imprudent to express his honest opinion of the non art. He looked around for something with which he could bean the total crone. All he could find was a coconut on the table next to him. He hefted that nut high over *the* nut.

"Wouldn't do that, cuddle cakes," Mavis admonished. "Might find yourself buck naked, posing for the cupid in the clouds above your cutie friend." She turned and stuck the paint brush into Roger's ear. "Yeah," she said, impressed by her inspiration. "Great idea! Take it off, baby, and zip over next to your pewee pal. I wanna get you in on the funzy, too!"

Roger's jaw, and the coconut, dropped to the floor. His face adopted the coloration of blood.

The witch stared at him with disbelief. "Ain't too intellectual, are you, boy?" she said. "Get them duds off, before I toss you, head first, into Mister Alligator Pit! Quick! My muse is fading!" She placed a paint smeared palm to the wall next to her. A portion of it snapped back and up, revealing an iron grille behind which crowded six seething alligators. They seemed to take an instant liking to Roger. Much to his intense dislike. She wiggled her fingers against the bars and the unregenerate grille crept up an inch. The alligators strained wildly to slink under it.

Roger stripped so fast the air hummed. He stood next to Wilkin with his hands in a protective manner. When Wilkin yanked his mitts away, Roger used his own hands to modestly cover himself.

The witch winced. "Boy," she said, "I ain't shy. Try and look like you got a big bow and arrow pointed at your slinky friend." She dabbed a moment at the tormented canvas. "Getting obscenely obese, aren't you!" she observed. "Got a big pretty navel, though; mother's side?"

Roger mumbled incoherently.

"Don't blush so, blubber butt, it's clashing with my masterpiece," Mavis warned. "I need a livid white." She made the grille rise an inch or two.

Roger turned white.

"That's my little snuggle-snot," Mavis approved. "Keep it that way. But don't you dare croak on me! I can't use a dead one." As she heartlessly assaulted the hapless canvas with vicious jabs, she muttered unkind remarks about Roger's body. In about ten eternal minutes, she stood back and adored her gleaming gift to the foul arts. "You can place your curious duds on now," she said. "I won't peek."

Wilkin pulled his pants on. "She ain't normal," he said, "that's all there is to that sad, squalid song! The queer bitch ain't even slightly near one fortieth normal!"

Roger tugged into his pajama bottoms and poked at the red paint in his ear. "Can she really spell us into squalling, limp-haired, pseudo-things?" he said. "Or is she just farting from her mouth?"

Wilkin sniffled for two minutes. "Yeah," he said. "She turned a teensy, three legged spider into that biggest alligator, there. That's when I kindly agreed to pose for her base pornography! You think she'll let us go?"

As he buttoned his pajama top, Roger watched the antique hag. She was putting the final touches on her painting. He was not the least interested in how he looked as cupid. "When you're ready," he whispered, "we'll make a mad dash for freedom. There must be a doorway out of here, somewhere, we can use."

Wilkin nodded and buckled his belt.

"Don't depart yet, precious children," Mavis said somberly. She threw her mixing board and brush on the floor. "It's time for dinner!"

Roger and Wilkin stiffened. Roger because of the fable of Hansel and Gretel. Wilkin because of a similar, but worse, true story.

"I always eat after I create a painting," Mavis said. She stepped over in two strides, moving like a disfigured phantom in a fast motion nightmare, and hooked her skinny, powerful arms around their shoulders before they could un-stiffen and wildly flee.

Roger could hardly breathe.

"What would you like?" Mavis asked, in a loving, yet psychotic, manner.

"Freedom!" Wilkin said, with a gasp.

"Don't be sassy," Mavis said, "or mommy will have to punish you into submission and a definite, humiliating attitude readjustment." She glowered at Roger and loosened her death grip on him. "You twinkle like a sensible chip off the old glod," she said. "What would you suggest for our Epicurean delight?"

Roasted Hag ass, Roger thought. But he didn't dare voice it. Instead, he decided to make the best of the odious situation. "How about fried chicken, mashed potatoes and pinto beans? With a stiff belt of gin as a chaser?" he was barely brave enough to say.

Mavis gave him a reproachful look. "I didn't imagine you were that type," she said. "Surprises are nice.

But, I'll have to read your deplorable, dweeb thoughts to conjure up what you suggested. We don't have it here. You from one of those tasteless foreign countries Al lied to me about?"

"You've never heard of it," Roger croaked. He was terrified she might find out about Earth and use her magic to take them both there. Then force him to marry her. The very thought of this fate worse than death made his bowels go dangerously slack.

"No doubt," Mavis said, in an air-headed manner. She dragged them to another room Roger had missed in his search for Wilkin. It was not his day all around. She kicked the door open and shoved the kidnapes in.

Roger and Wilkin were astonished. The glare of the phosphorescent ceiling revealed a gorgeous dining room. The walls were covered with brown velvet and lined with towering, ornate book shelves. Nauseating, lurid paintings hung between the book cases over small wooden tables upon which sat many tasteless statues cast of solid glod.

Roger assumed the canvasses had been perverted by the witch.

In the center of the floor, which was covered by a green, ultra-pile carpet, was a figure-eight-shaped, wooden dinner table. Chilled bottles of gin sat beside bejeweled, glod goblets. Glod plates were heaped with steaming fried chicken, mashed potatoes and pinto beans. Glod flatware rested on purple silk napkins.

Mavis fussed them into their glod-filigree-embellished wooden chairs. She attempted to look fetching. When they did not respond, she released the rubber ball from her hog-like teeth and threw up her hands. "It ain't easy looking nice when you're as homely as the insides of a horse," she confessed.

Roger agreed with fervor but wisely said nothing. Instead, he opened his gin and poured a stiff belt into his goblet. He had suffered too much today. The entire universe, God, and even simpering Satan, owed him a merciful form of anesthesia, or euthanasia.

"I thought that was for chasers?" Wilkin said. He was afraid Roger would put on a screaming drunk and be useless in any probably insanely, futile, escape attempt.

"If he drinks enough of it," Mavis said, with an affected girlish giggle, "he'll be a chaser! A girl chaser! Chasing prissy, kissy, little me!" Syrup thick silence replied. "Guffaw it up, boys," she suggested, with the tone of a funeral orator. "It's the only thing keeping you alive!"

Roger giggled vacuously into his gin, then set-to on his food. He desperately hoped Alvisor would find and free them in some way, like a dyspeptic Jesus leading upside down souls out of a cartoon hell. Preferably before Roger went utterly insane from Mavis's god awful looks!

***

Halfway through choking down his raspberry-flavored, orange hued mashed potatoes, Roger imagined he heard the familiar rasp of Alvisor's voice. It seemed to be coming from beside a bookcase behind Mavis. But there was nothing there, just the wall. Or was it the wall? If walls possessed bloodshot eyes, it was, indeed, the wall. But he didn't believe walls had bloodshot eyes. Of course, on *this* planet, and in a witch's home— He winked at the wall, hoping it was actually Alvisor, and not just his gin, and slowly finished his nauseating spuds.

Mavis was retelling the dynamic events which led up to her fortuitous birth. She slapped Roger on the neck with her gleaming glod fork. "Wasn't *that* a kick in the old, tile covered, pantaloons!" she said. She attacked a hunk of newly conjured skunk meat. "You boys ain't been to sociable, and I'm getting right peeved. I'm doing you an angelic favor by letting you live and keeping you with me forever. Not to mention risking my own priceless hide by disobeying *The Monster's* orders. So you'd better friendly up or—"

Alvisor appeared atop the dinner table. He had a long, bulky, brown-paper-wrapped bundle under one arm. His trembling right hand was clutching a bust of Grato The Administrator. He cracked the witch on the head once.

Roger was certain he saw old Grato screw up his gloden face with revulsion just before the bust struck home.

Mavis slumped into her potatoes with her fork handle sticking up her bulbous nose.

Alvisor dropped the bust on the carpet. A mistake for which he would never forgive himself. He leaped from the table, grabbed Wilkin by the nose and ran for freedom. The old magician still had the paper bundle.

Roger considered his grandiose plans for revenge against Mavis. He decided the absence of his fine, gentle and precious self from the mega creepy crone would be punishment enough. Then he decided to punch her on the face a few times, simply for good measure. Before he could finish his wind up, Mavis began swearing herself to consciousness. He suddenly realized he was alone with the horrid witch. He was stricken with a stark terror no man before could have known! He fled the room so hard his eyes bulged out of his head in an attempt to pull him faster along the hallway. He heard Wilkin's faint bawling down an unfamiliar corridor and was soon six steps behind Alvisor and the dwarf. He sighted a tall crack in the rock; the back door. He raced for it like a miser after money.

Far away, like the bellowing of an anguished Wedsell lost in an argyle sock factory, Mavis's voice rose in crescendo, laying a chant through the air: "Walls! Walls! Close in tight! Return all interlopers to my sight!"

The exit shut with a reverberating crunching of rock, belching the triad into the rolling desert. They hot footed it across the sands without a moments hesitation. Life threatening dehydration was supremely preferable to Miss Mavis.

***

The afternoon sun spread weird light across the wrinkled dunes. Alvisor dropped his bundle and plopped flat on his back on the warm sand. Roger and Wilkin joined him.

"How the hell did you finesse us into and out of that mess?" Roger demanded.

"Well," Alvisor said. "I sighted them there Sweet and Nut Roots like I wanted and got all excited. When I pulled the first one out of the ground, I bonked myself upside the forehead and went down for the long count.

"When I came to, I filled my saddlebags with roots and hied myself back to where I'd left my great friends. By then, of course, you had sadly disappeared, without your horses!

"I sat my spiffy but distraught self down on the road to think. Suddenly I recognized I was again, tragically, in Miss Mavis's Girdle! I knowed, in an instant, what had transpired to you, because, numerous years ago, I met your former dinner hostess here. She was quite a womern *then*." He wiped his eyes and nose on the hem of his robe. "We might a had it fine if she hadn't a wanted to get married. I told her to go kiss a rabid Grommit and lit out for safer territories. The last I heard from her was a

curse what curled my socks and warped my drawers.

"A Wedsell chased our fine horses back toward Devil's Foot, so I was forced to hike all the way to her rear entrance. You guys are fortunate I still had her back door key. I raided her pantry, then searched for you two. We're *all* lucky I remembered my Chameleon Spell, and how to shield my voice from all but you, Roger. There's no telling what unspeakables she might have performed on you."

"Or what *The Monster* might do to us when he finds out she didn't do us in!" Wilkin said, wiping his eyes with his thumbs.

Chapter 16
Scout It Out

"Stop, driver!"

The coach swayed to a halt, its wheels sinking deep into the sand. Even with the assistance of magic, they were making very poor speed this morning.

The Monster telepathically mesmerized the stallions to stillness. "Damn those men!" he said. "They have escaped Mavis! Norgrum and Mavis will regret betraying me, in butter sauce, for a very long time!"

"Was it the unnatural luck again, master?"

"The magician's power!" The Monster said. "He has managed to utilize his confetti brain thrice so far. I wish I had not placed The Traitor's Stone on his convoluted forehead!"

"But, master!" the driver exclaimed, unwisely. "If you hadn't, the old Magus wouldn't have told you where Aleron is!"

"And, if I hadn't shit a big, reeking turd," The Monster roared, with anger, "*you* wouldn't be here!"

"Please, master, you promised you wouldn't remind me!"

The doors swept open and the steps unfolded on both sides of the coach. The driver hastened down and stood at the right hand door.

"They are nearby, to our right," The Monster said. "Scout them out and return swiftly."

The driver scurried across the dunes as quickly as the loose, hot sand permitted.

When his rapscallion toady was out of sight, The Monster vacated the coach. He was covered by his ebony habit and its loose hood. He raised his gloved hands to the sky. "Powers wax; hide our tracks," he rumbled.

The deep trail of hoof prints and wagon wheel ruts filled in as though an unfelt wind were blowing the sand.

***

The driver made his way back to the coach. After he caught his breath, he said: "They are proceeding toward The Great Mountain Range, master!"

The Monster raised his hands above the sporty luggage rack. "Powers wax; hide slave's tracks!" After a short pause, he said: "Ply the Light. Ease my plight. As we go, no tracks show!" He climbed into the jiggling, complaining coach. "Mount, driver! We *must* reach The Cow's Mouth before they do. There are things, therein, which I can utilize to destroy them, once each day, for as long as time exists!" The stairs folded up correctly and the doors snapped shut. He un-mesmerized the stallions. "On, you recycled turnip!"

Chapter 17

The Cow's Mouth

"Oh, Budda!" Wilkin pleaded. "Pluck my soul into your, glittering, rich hands and spare me the ordeal of the snot damned *Cow's Mouth*!"

The trio shaded themselves with red umbrellas as they trudged over the smoldering dunes. The Great Mountain Range was a dark wall before them.

The package Alvisor brought from Mavis's house contained the three bumbershoots, some meager strings of jerky, and a small skin of water.

"Is The Cow's Mouth *really* a threat?" Roger said meekly. He stopped for no reason other than increasing fear.

"It's filled with wicked magic," Wilkin said, with a very small voice. "Uncontrolled magic, with a devil-may-care, but twisted mind of its own making!"

"Wh—what's so bad about that?" Roger said. The fear was now clutching at the nape of his fat neck. He sat down to hide the weakness the terror caused in his shaking knees.

"It used to be a punishment place," Alvisor said. "Once in a while, a brave magician, witch or drunk sorcerer would try to defeat the strongest wizard. He would strip them of their puny powers and cast them into The Cow's Mouth. Then he'd let their own magic loose in there to punish them. Aleron hurled the last despot wizard in there thirty years ago."

"How can we protect ourselves?" Roger begged.

"Get in! Get out!" Alvisor said. He was grievously displeased at his inability to offer comfort and potent advice.

***

They slogged on until the mountain range filled the horizons. The individual peaks were composed of multi-colored stone which reflected the glare of the punishing sun in all the glorious colors of the rainbow, belying the threat they posed. A great pass cut through the center of the range and the yellow sands of The WharlWash Desert churned frantically about its mouth, despite the absence of winds.

Roger thought this was a gratuitously scary phenomenon. "Do you think The Monster's been through here yet?" he said. "He'd have to leave the road to reach The Cow's Mouth. Wouldn't he be slowed in the sand, even with eerie magic? I haven't seen any tracks since we left Mavis's."

"Then, that slimy booger probably ain't been here," Wilkin said.

"Yeah, but he might use his magic to hide his tracks," Roger said.

"What do you think, Alvisor?" Wilkin said.

"I don't know. Just keep your peepers peeled."

***

Much to the dislike of the trio, they crossed through an area littered with the bleached bones of man and dwarf. Even someone as rudely huge as Bellus was there, stripped of his flesh by the scavengers and elements; looking like a critic in the nude.

***

The intrepid trio finally reached the ominous pass. The uncanny actions of the sand ceased as though a switch had been thrown.

This reminded Roger of the way a cat becomes statue-still the instant before it pounces on an unwary rodent. Then his touch of hope about getting home vanished.

The Cow's Mouth was blocked by a shimmering, translucent barrier. It stretched from the peaks towering on their left, to the peaks looming on their right.

Alvisor pressed his hands hard against the magic shield but it did not give.

Wilkin sighed happily.

Roger was just sad.

"I guess that settles that," Alvisor said. "The Monster's been here already. Used to be, anybody fool enough could go into The Cow's Mouth. And out, if he wasn't marked by the big sorcerer, or killed by something inside. Now, The Monster's got it closed off completely, creating a key, to get through, that only *he* knows about. I guess we don't get in."

"You sure it's The Monster's work?" Roger said.

"Yeah," Alvisor said. "Nobody else has a reason to keep people out of the Cow's Mouth. The short-eyed so and so!"

Roger shut his eyes, rubbed them tiredly, then stared angrily at the pass.

A huge, ghostly, gray hand formed in the air in front of the barrier.

Roger was so startled he gasped several times, sounding like an ancient locomotive straining to travel a nearly vertical rail bed.

Wilkin fainted at the uncanny noise.

The hand pointed to a rock on the left side of the pass and, in slow motion, pressed it into the sand.

"What is it, boy?" Alvisor demanded. "What do you see?"

The spectral hand vanished.

Roger's mind cleared and he shook himself.

"What is it, boy?" Alvisor demanded. "What do you see?"

"A phantom hand pushed that rock into the sand," Roger whispered, "and disappeared! Do you think *that's* the key?"

Roger and Alvisor carefully approached the stone.

Wilkin came awake and glanced around in pleasurable ignorance. He toddled to where Roger and Alvisor were talking. It appeared they did not want him in on the rap, so he decided to take another nap. A voluntary one. He sat down on a rock at Alvisor's feet.

"Wilkin!" Roger warned. "No!"

The dwarf sensed wrongness and it felt like a wind swept him backwards as he disappeared from the stone.

Roger and Alvisor watched Wilkin's silhouette appear behind the magic barrier and then vanish.

Thoughts rocketed through Roger's mind. Some were lewd. Some were crude. But the strongest was: Friend! "Wilkin!" he shouted. "We're coming!" He jumped onto the stone and disappeared.

Alvisor froze. Then he was hit by something approximating what Roger had felt. Mostly, he didn't want to be alone in the soulless desert. He leaped onto the key stone, and in half a heart beat, was inside The Cow's Mouth Prison Pass.

Chapter 18

The Forest of Corrupted Darkness

"Oh, fickle life!" Alvisor lamented. He pressed his long nose against the barrier, which was transparent from the inside.

The magic of the barrier had blown Roger and Wilkin into a sand dune. They struggled free and joined the unhappy magician.

"We've left our umbrellas, our water and most of the jerky behind. There ain't no key rock here, so we can't go out and recover our stuff," Alvisor said. "I wouldn't bet counterfeit glod on our chances of screaming through this spell-infested hell unharmed."

Although the trio could see the morning sun, The Cow's Mouth was semi-dark.

Rashly ignoring this ominous portent, and casting fear aside, Roger waved his friends more deeply into The Cow's Mouth.

The steep sides of the pass were composed of depressing, slippery, un-climbable gray granite, rather than the cheerful multi-colored stone seen outside. Dry sand and ancient Wedsell holes spread on and on until they crashed into the horizon. There was no evidence the freaky Monster, or any other living being, had passed this way.

A sluggish breeze prowled against their sweat-soaked backs. A presence seemed to be everywhere, listening to and evaluating them.

No doubt, Roger thought, planning something I and my pals won't appreciate.

***

The dunes and Wedsell holes seemed to crawl by like drugged snails.

Roger kept looking over his shoulder every few paces. He was still feeling that—presence.

***

At dead noon, the trio encountered a brooding forest which blocked their path and continued up both sides of the pass, incredibly growing out of the slick granite. Although there was no breeze, the O-shaped, black leaves fluttered without cease. The ebony trunks resembled all the misshapen monsters in all the B horror movies with which Roger had unwisely cluttered his impressionable mind.

Tall and thin.

Bowed, fat and twisted.

Short, grasping and demented.

Wilkin stared, frightened, into the unnatural solid appearing darkness between the gnarled trees.

"We *have* to strut through it," Alvisor said, with self-assuring gruffness.

A blood clotting scream, such as a ghoul with terminal gas would utter, escaped from the heart of the forest. A chorus of continuing alto, bass and concert-saw screams followed.

"Wh—what's making those noises?" Roger said, his voice weak with fear.

"The souls of the magicians, witches and wizards trapped in The Forest of Corrupted Darkness for truly malevolent crimes against society and the old Great Sorcerers. They're probably in there, too," Alvisor said.

Roger sat down on the sand and put his head between his knees. "Can they hurt us?" he whispered.

"Ahh, only if they—"

"Only if they get a chance!" Wilkin shouted. "And just spitting into that forest gives them one hell of a fat, juicy chance!"

The screams were coming fast and thick now, louder, then softer, in a repeating rhythm, just at the edge of the forest. Amorphous lights sprang up between the thick-trunked trees, the thin-trunked trees and the Ogre-shaped trees, and began blinking red, green, blue, yellow and orange, over and over.

Roger stood up. He struggled to avert his eyes from the lights, but his body seemed to turn to stone. Beside him, Wilkin and Alvisor were rooted in their tracks.

The lights swirled toward one another until they became one, shining like a small, varicolored sun. The

multi-light warmed the trio. It called to them, soothed them, and slyly made them happy.

The trio shuffled toward the forest.

Solid arms of colored light, with long, sparkling fingers, extended from the sides of the multi-orb and reached out from under the black, circular leaves. The fingers strained, touched, then began to encircle Roger's upheld, limp wrists.

Roger screamed in his mind and blinked his bugged out, bloodshot eyes.

The multi-light sighed like a thousand dying martyrs. Without sound, heat or shock wave, it exploded into tiny, colored globes, each of which faded from the darkness between the trees. The screams ceased and the leaves stopped fluttering.

Roger un-stiffened. He leaped back from the nearest Troll-shaped tree. His eyes ached and his head was buzzing like an electric razor snorkeling under atomic heavy water.

Wilkin and Alvisor were just beginning to awaken from the hypnosis.

"What did you do?" Alvisor said.

"Blinked my eyes," Roger admitted. "Wonder why they gave up?"

"Didn't give up, boy," Alvisor said, with uncharacteristic realization. "They was channeling their nasty mystic energy through runt's left eye, out his right, into your left, out your right, into my left, out my right, and back into their malevolent selves.

"When you blinked, you broke the psychic circuit, releasing all their misbegotten powers into the air. It'll take them spiritual bloodsuckers hundreds of years to regain so much energy."

"Do you think The Monster had anything to do with their receiving power?" Roger asked.

"You can bet your third leg on it," Alvisor said. "There's no way of telling how many other traps he might of set for us. We'll have to be very careful, as usual. Which is an understatement, at best."

"Fine situation," Roger complained. "If The Monster's not behind us, trying to kill us, he's ahead of us, trying to kill us!"

"It's not my frivolous fault he wants Aleron's magic," Alvisor said defensively. "If I'd a known The Monster would be involved, I'd a stayed at home, in a comfort pail, shaking hard!"

"Me included!" Wilkin avowed.

"At any rate," Alvisor said. "It's safe to go through the forest now, without fear of those twisted magic souls sucking the spiritual sap and life force out of our cute, but helpless bodies."

They did.

And they did not.

***

The other side of The Forest of Corrupted Darkness revealed only more bleak desert, rocks and Wedsell holes.

Roger was incensed. He snarled at Alvisor and wandered a little ahead of his friends. He slapped his palm to his forehead. He wanted to think of something useful. But all he could manage was a mental image of himself lying on a marble slab. A morgue bed. A stiff pedestal. He diverted his mind to an inspection of the desolation again. His sad heart rose into his throat. Far off, glistening even in the semi darkness of The Cow's Mouth, was another barrier!

***

The travelers pressed their sweaty palms and runny noses against the long, transparent shield. They resembled joyless monkeys in a cruel Zoo.

Alvisor snorted until his beard trembled.

On the misty horizon, there was a faint hint of green. This was where the blistering desert ended and The Enchanted Swamp began.

"How do we get out?" Wilkin said. "Maybe it's got a key stone, too?"

"Do you see one?" Roger said.

Wilkin looked hopefully to the left and right, where the huge barrier met with the mountain ranges. He saw only flat, dry sand. "No," he admitted, slumping his shoulders.

"Maybe we can't open it!" Roger mumbled. "Trapped in a barbecue pit, forever!"

"Before we entered, I knowed The Monster changed the front barrier," Alvisor said. "I should have figured he'd shut the rear shield after him so it wouldn't let us out! I doubt it, but try closing your eyes again, boy. Maybe you'll see a second key!"

Roger was more than willing. He closed and opened his eyes several dozen times for several dozen minutes, in fact. But all he saw was Alvisor. He did not notice he saw the old, red haired prune when his eyes were closed as well as when they were open. "No good," he said bleakly.

"Uhhhh!" Alvisor said. "I can't think of an escape! My poor mind won't work!"

"It never has!" Wilkin said angrily.

Roger brightened up. He tapped Alvisor on the forehead. "What's this cussed shield made of, swami?" he asked.

"Magic," Alvisor mumbled.

"What's magic made of?" Roger asked.

"Mostly thought," Alvisor said, almost interested. "Why?"

"Thought is, maybe, electromagnetic energy," Roger said, knowing as little about what he was raving as did his desperately hopeful pals. "And energy can be short circuited. Why don't you short-circuit this puny shield?"

Alvisor's eyes popped in and out for a moment. "How's that, again?" he asked, like a bully insulted by a coward.

"The barrier is thought," Roger said. "You can use your magic thought to break it. Drill a hole into it—"

"Use my stinging fists on your hollow head if you don't grip hold of yourself," Alvisor said. "The thought what went into that there shield was increased by magic book incantations what I don't know. Plus old potions I ain't aware of. And I don't know what else! I can't think it down. But—maybe—no—I almost—if I only had some water," he said, with a moan, "I could whip up *some* kinder escape!" He angrily kicked at the smoldering sand.

Water sprang out of the resulting cavity the way panhandlers spring out of gutters to chase after disgusted wealthy pedestrians.

Wilkin began to bawl. He was afraid he would shrink.

"Move away from the water, stupid," Roger said, like a typical loving parent.

Wilkin considered the words. He strutted a few feet from the forming pool, then sat down. "Gee!" he said, with admiration and wonder at Roger's wise suggestion. He began fanning himself with his hands and feet to get dry.

Alvisor waded into the pool and sat down. He began dipping his hands into the water and flapping his beard around in the startled air.

Water flooded over Roger's ankles. He watched Alvisor, in horror. "He's gone," he said, mourning for the aged magician. "He's whacked out of his gourd. Mentally ruptured!"

The water began to spew. It spread over the sand like army ants over spilled honey.

Wilkin began to run from the waves.

Alvisor floated atop the water with his legs in a lotus position.

Roger was trapped on a disappearing dune. "We'll all drown!" he shouted angrily. "We'll all horribly drown, just because you wanted a drink of water! You could have waited, Mr. Pygmy Will!"

Alvisor was oblivious to Roger's railing. He was whipping his beard faster and faster around his head, snapping his whiskers like a whip on each turn. The slow tide carried him toward the shimmering barrier.

The water caught Wilkin by the legs and pulled him down under its advancing wetness.

Roger's shrinking dune collapsed on one side, dropping him into the cool dark water.

Alvisor's beard began to whistle as it snapped and streaked even faster around his head. He floated closer to the barrier and—kerpow—his beard tips exploded against it. Lightning crackled! Catnip-scented smoke flew and the shield suffered a momentary, horizontal split, from mountain range to mountain range!

Bearing Alvisor, Wilkin and Roger, the gurgling water rushed out of the insidious Cow's Mouth. The sun parched sands instantly absorbed the miserable waves, leaving the startled, but grateful trio flat on their backs and catching their breath under the wondering evening sky.

Chapter 19

The Enchanted Swamp

"Do we gotta go on?" Wilkin begged.

The Enchanted Swamp was surrounded by purple grass and green, leather-textured rocks. It was dark, hulking and forbidding, even under the morning sun. It grasped at the reluctant trio with multicolored fronds, X-shaped leaves, giant flowers and naked dolls painted to look like buxom women.

"Yeah," Roger said. "Alvisor's got a spell or two. That'll give us *some* protection."

"But, you have to believe in me, boy!" Alvisor said. He wrung his dish water reddened hands. "Magic and magicians have to be believed *in* before they can really be effective." His shoulders slumped and a tear smeared one of his weathered cheeks. "No one's believed in me, or my magic, for a long, sad, lonely, painful time now, boy. That's the real reason none of my spells works proper. That's why I'm forced to be a quack."

Roger patted the Magus on the back. "I'll believe in you from this day forward." he promised.

Alvisor's face lighted up like sewer water reflecting

sunrise. "You do that, boy," he crowed, "and nothing will touch us! Suddenly, I'm remembering some pretty vicious spells of protection!" He bustled about, hunting up the necessary ingredients for the coming conjuration.

Wilkin watched, screwing his face up with un-disguised doubt.

"Can I assist you with your curious work, Mr. Shaman?" Roger asked.

"Dig over there and bring me what you find," Alvisor said eagerly. He ripped dried leaves off several types of ugly weeds, crushed them between his hands, and threw the bits on the ground.

Roger grabbed a couple of rocks and started excavating the soft earth at the indicated spot. He uncovered a sizable green root which looked nauseatingly like a gleaming glob of snot. "What's this for?" he asked precariously.

"That there is your basic Mystic Power Root!" the comus shouted. He was overcome with the excitement of conjuring, plus the prospect of actual success. "It makes them powers what be, ride high and snap tight!" He wrestled the snotty looking tuber out of the earth, laid it beside the crushed leaves and jumped on it.

A crimson-eyed banshee, in stunning, diaphanous blue apparel, hissed out of the end of the root like a genie from a bottle, screaming like the utter alto bitch she was.

"We're gonna be stuck with Miss Sweetness fer a while," Alvisor confided in Roger. "This root's her home, and she'll not leave until we're finished with it." He jumped harder on the shiny tuber. It blooged out some yellow juice which soaked into the crushed leaves and the grassy earth. "It's all yourn again, dear," he said. He kicked the root across the grass to the howling bitch.

The banshee threw a pink toilet stool lid at the Magus. She vaporized, hissed into her slimy home, and caused the tuber to replant itself with a sickening sqwug sound.

"Isn't that rather mean?" Roger inquired.

Alvisor flipped one of the green rocks over, uncovering a Fezz Lizard. He grabbed the beast and squeezed its orange, spiked tail until a drop of its muddy sweat plopped onto the root juice sodden ground. "Naw," he said. "Banshees get used to it, after a hundred years. They even, secretly, look forward to it. They mark it down on their Occult Calenders, and eagerly wait for it to occur." He released the lizard.

The reptile mewed monstrously at the shaman, messed on the toe of one of his boots, and waddled indignantly into the swamp.

"Much obliged," the magician said fondly, to the Fezz. He toed the turd into the wet spot and leaned, at a forty-five degree angle, toward Roger. "Magic work's sickening, ain't it?" he said, with a gasp.

Roger, half numb from the stink, only nodded.

Alvisor found a stick. He stirred and poked at the mess and wet sod. The violet grass uprooted and the concoction meshed into a ball of reeking mud. "*That, my google eyed friends, is that,*" he said.

The ball of homemade sludge gave vent to a crunching like monsters eating cadavers. It began bubbling and issuing a reddish-green gas reminiscent of rotting fish. Two black eyes appeared and stared at Roger with malcontent.

"Damn!" Alvisor said. "We're in for more and more trouble!"

"How's that?" Wilkin said, with worry.

"Turn on your brain, malfunct," Alvisor said. "This earth's been changed magically, recently, no doubt by *The Monster*. My spell should have worked, but it got warped. He'll beat us to Aleron, for sure, now!"

"Not if we out run him," Roger said, with determination. "I don't care how much magic he has. He can't take a coach up that mountain you mentioned. He'll have to climb, just like us."

"Yeah," Alvisor said. "But he's on the other side of the Swamp. We're here. And the agent I just concocted might follow after us, with evil notions of a bygone, but not mourned for, era!"

"Psssst!" an Enchanted Tree said. It had large, child-like blue eyes. "None of my fellow Enchanted Trees will harm you." It shrugged its leafy branches. "Of course, this don't mean them ounce-brained flowers will leave you in peace, once you traipse in here!"

"Watch it, knothole face!" yelled a purplish blossom. It was further inside the swamp. "I happen to know you're a filthy fertilizer addict, and can't gum a postage stamp!"

"You wouldn't be so stupid if you'd leave them nitrates alone," the tree charged. "They cause splotchy leaves and brain damage. But you and your degenerate sort gotta get your insane thrills, no matter what!"

"Somebody ought to chop that foul, reeking mouth right out of you!" the bloom retorted.

"You ought to get your petals trimmed!" the tree snarled. "You look like a Mescalara Bush!"

"You skanky, seed fetishist, weeds shut up and let a decent flora sleep!" roared a Giant Fern. It was rapidly blinking its multiple red eyes in rage.

"Keep your frondy mouth out of this, you perennial scum!" the tree and the flower screamed.

"Come on," Roger said, with disgust. "Let's jet through this place before they remember we're here!"

Full of misgivings and banana and onion jerky, the trio delved into the enormous, cacophonous swamp.

The Enchanted Plants and the sticky mud ringed only the outer section of the discordant marsh. They gave way to regular HackHell flora.

The black triangular leaves of the gnarled and warped trees formed a canopy so thick it increasingly blocked out the comforting sunlight.

***

It fell so dark, Wilkin's eyes emitted long beams of yellow light, revealing the orange moss and old leaves carpeting the damp earth.

This amazed the happy dwarf as much as it did his frightened-of-the-booger-filled-dark companions.

"Real handy, them peepers is," Alvisor purred, like he knew Wilkin's eyes would illuminate the way.

"Keep your hypocrisy to yourself!" Wilkin said.

They approached an area where several human skeletons sat, or laid, half buried by millions of tiny red flowers.

"I ain't no dirt-mouthed hypocrite!" Alvisor said. He began waving his hands in a grand fashion.

"Lord!" Roger shouted. "Here comes extemporaneous hubris!"

Alvisor and Wilkin stopped, in shock.

Some of the flowers wilted.

"He's a educated man!" Alvisor exclaimed, with awe. He grabbed his beard and began gnawing its tips.

"*Real* edicated," Wilkin sagely agreed.

"This changes things," the magician gravely pronounced. "Educated men is weird."

"They always has ideas," Wilkin said.

"Always asking sex questions on job forms and *census* sheets," Alvisor added.

"Oh, peas!" Roger said. "Go to hell! Education is not a disease or a crime!"

"You ain't been to *our* schools," Wilkin monotoned. A red glow came into his eyes, dimming their lights. "Oh! The regimented horrors of the unspeakable years of being beated with the meat of books for five days a wicked week! It wasn't nothing to do to the free soul of an innocent man-child. So mean," he cooed. "So black-kneed, trashy, nasty mean! Filled a child's head with useless facts what couldn't even help him shit his pants in reflex action!" He gasped as if he were dying. "My, damn!" he said. "Them well-worn memories do require a lot of your time and energy. Not to mention their taking over your unwilling mind." He sighed like the only angel allowed to sit next to God, then fell blissfully silent. The red glow faded from his eyes, allowing them to regain their bright shine. The skeletons and flowers sparkled around him.

"What do you remember, Alvisor?" Roger said, wistfully.

"Them women—"

Roger slapped a hand over the Magus's mouth.

Alvisor shoved the fat mitt away. "Them women what own the Library," he continued, "told me about this place!" He conjured up a fish sandwich. "The Dell of Remembrance!" he shouted. "Now I recalls, quite clear! Strong psychic energy starts it off." He offered a bite of his sandwich to his friends.

Wilkin took one as he happily recalled when his seven foot tall mother used to sculpt real boss sandwiches.

"They claims you get to recollecting. You become happy. And you just sit around in a joy remembering all your pleasureful past, until you get ate up by a *thing*. Or until you starves to death. I guess The Monster set it going when he passed through," Alvisor concluded, cheerfully. He sat on the backbone of a skeleton and nibbled his sandwich.

Roger scratched his head. Then he scratched his own head. "Why doesn't it affect me?" he asked, jealously.

Alvisor and Wilkin almost became sad. "Ain't got no happy memories, I guess," they chorused.

A peal of psychotic demon laughter startled the fab trio and snapped the seductive spell of the insidious Dell.

Roger hugged himself.

Alvisor dropped his sandwich and leaped to his feet, peering intently into the far darkness, in the direction from which they had come.

Wilkin desperately tried to go unconscious, but fell down and bumped his head.

Chapter 20

The Blackness

The laugh sounded again, only much nearer. A giant, shimmering shape of Blackness could be seen gliding between the trees. It was darker than the ebony shadows, and it was pulling a gleaming, silver laugh-machine on little white wheels. As it floated toward the frightened trio, it pitched over onto its side for no apparent reason. It righted itself with a loud, sacred oath, then angrily jostled the laugh machine, lamely trying to blame it for the accident.

"Bull shit!" Roger said. "You don't even have quality ghosts on your world!" He looked amazed. "I said *that*?" he wondered aloud. Their brush with Zukove clawed its way out of his memory and he began to regret his rash words. He started trembling.

"Yeah," the Blackness sniveled. It stopped between two trees a few yards from the trio. The distance and the darkness obscured it so well, even Wilkin's eye lights did not reveal its looks. "And that weren't too kind a slur to utter about a feller who does the best he can with anachronistic implements." It raised a clown-sized foot of darkness and kicked the laugh machine. The device cackled raucously. "It's a rebellious mother, too!" the Blackness rumbled.

The machine was bejeweled and covered with fascinating knobs and gears.

Wilkin started toward the contrivance.

Roger grabbed the dwarf by the throat, Alvisor by the beard, and ran hell-bent-for-leather away from the Blackness.

A hive of red spiders dropped to the ground the trio vacated. They found Alvisor's strings of jerky and his fine fish sandwich and ravenously consumed them.

The Blackness laughed like the malignancy it had accidentally been born, by Alvisor, to be. "I'll catch you and slow-motion kill you into little, painful, bloody pieces just as The Monster would!" it promised. It abandoned its laugh machine, and its spiders, and flashed into the air like a wind blown, decaying bird.

Roger was hampered by Wilkin's constant tripping over roots, rocks and flowers. He hefted the dwarf onto his shoulders, grabbed the wheezing, aged Magus around the waist, and forced himself to run even faster under the added weight.

As they mazed their way through the trees of the quagmire, the flowers and moss gave way to grass.

"Leave me behind, boy!" Alvisor said, with a gasp. "It ain't right you should die on a world not your own!"

"Shut up!" Roger ordered. "I see some light ahead!"

Alvisor stumbled over a root and Roger was pulled to his knees.

Wilkin screamed as he was jerked off Roger's aching shoulders.

Roger pushed the shaman behind a tree, spun around, and blundered into the hard chest of the Blackness.

The demon was squeezing Wilkin between its big, shiny black hands.

Roger grabbed up a stick and jabbed it, with all his might and rage, against the slippery chest of the conjury. The plastic skin punctured and the creature began deflating. A sobbing, misty substance fled from the nostrils of the rat-like head and harmlessly dispersed into the shadows. When enough air escaped, the hands lost their grip and Wilkin dropped like a bomb.

Roger caught the short man, with out injury to either of them, and laid the dwarf out on the grass. "Alvisor!" he yelled, urgently.

The magician loomed close, uncapped a small bottle, and poured its contents into the dwarf's slack mouth. Wilkin gulped like a sump pump. He hollered like a stepped on bullfrog. His eyes beamed like yellow beacons in a barrel filled with mirrors. He leaped to his feet, delivering a kick to Alvisor's knees. "I'd a come out of it in another moment, even if you hadn't brutalized me with monster piss!" he shouted. He gaped at the deflated Blackness, then stared at something sitting beside it. His teeth shone like gallstones polished by bile. "Where'd you get the beer?" he said.

Alvisor turned pink, like a child caught with a hand in a cookie jar. "My spell worked," he bragged. "Just called it right up." But it had been a fear accident while he was desperately rummaging through his stuffed-up head for a magical defense against the Blackness.

The cans of cold beer were in a bushel basket. The trio carried their booty to the edge of a huge clearing. This was cut in half by a towering hedge, behind which loomed a short, rocky mountain. Immediately before them, many logs and a lot of rocks lay on damp, ebon earth. They found the longest log they could, sat down facing the hedge-row, and opened a can of beer apiece by biting into the tops.

"Funny how your fine, occult spells work only by accident," Wilkin muttered. "Must be because your head only works by accident."

"Aw, go boil your eyes, you squatty monster teat," Alvisor said. "Can't accept nothing on face value. Don't know why I brung you along. Would've been better off with a sack of grade Z Wedsell Droppings."

"Go suck yourself," Wilkin said. He threw a bent can past Roger's nose and barely missed Alvisor. He opened another can, grinned at Roger, and lapsed into silence.

To his surprise, Roger downed four beers without pausing. Because he was not used to drinking, they affected him quickly. In fact, he was crying into his current can. It wasn't easy being hero brave. He was still shaking from his encounter with The Blackness.

Alvisor opened another can with his teeth. He saw there were no more in the basket. "We have to celebrate," he said.

"What for?" Wilkin said. "You didn't have the foresight to conjure up a can opener. My teeth hurt!" A can of beer materialized in front of him. He grabbed it and bit into the top.

Alvisor's spell was classier than he thought. This pleased him as much as crowns please kings.

"Can't you conjure these damn cans away?" Roger said. A ring of them was hovering around his head. "And stop them from appearing every time I turn around!"

"Hell," Alvisor said, "I'm surrounded by pink-assed perfectionists." He kicked a pile of empty cans, scattering them far, and marginally wide. "At least I managed to turn this wet stuff almost nonintoxicating," he said. "And we still gotta celebrate."

"Again," the dwarf mentioned, in off color tones, "what for?"

A gleam entered Alvisor's eyes. He pointed with his feet; his hands were inconvenienced by cans of beer. "Because, right up there, on top of that ol' mountain," he said, "lies the stronghold of Aleron, true, effective Magician and Loan Shark."

Roger looked happy through the ring of cans.

"Now we gotta climb a mountain!" Wilkin raved. "And slay, maybe, twelve thousand paprika eating Dragons! Plus a cord or two of One-Eyed Turnpikes! Then a couple million creeping, Giant Mobsters! *And,* maybe, a hellish Turd! *Or* two! *Or* slavering, half Right Wing-half Left Wing Hypocrites *and* animated Turkey Bones! *All* of what are supposed to *guard* his place!" He put his head between his knees and gurgled with impressive intensity.

Alvisor shoved an unopened can of beer away. It returned and attempted to open itself against his upper teeth. He smashed the can with a rock, soaking the ground with the clear, bubbly beer. "No," he said airily. His normal state. "Them's just legends. We'll probably not even *see* anything of the sort. Not even in your feverish, psycho dreams, Wilkin."

Roger turned the basket upside down, plucked the hovering cans out of the air and placed them under it.

Alvisor reluctantly reversed the beer spell and the trio headed toward the mountain. They penetrated the thick hedges backwards to protect their eyes. When they were through, the branches snapped back into place and appeared as if they had never been moved. The trio turned around and froze.

"Oh *hell*!" Roger said. "He's waiting for us. Let's die now, by our own, frenzied, hands, it'll surely hurt less than what he's probably about to do!"

Wilkin struggled head first against the hedges, attempting to force himself through to safety.

Alvisor grabbed the dwarf by the seat of the pants and

pointed him toward the great, glistening coach. "Use them round, bloodshot balls in your head and see that coach!" Alvisor ordered. "Notice anything?"

"Yeah," Wilkin whimpered, "any one of them hirsute horses could swallow me alive, sideways!"

"Notice the driver?" Alvisor ordered.

Wilkin and Roger looked hard.

Wilkin shrugged. "He's maybe, dead?" he said. "And so are them decadently expensive stallions?"

"Petrified," Roger corrected. "Like the bandits. *The Monster* doesn't need him any more. *Or* the horses."

Alvisor put Wilkin down. "Right," he said. "So, now he's alone. He's climbing somewhere in those rocks. Unless we're lucky. Maybe he's had a killer fall."

"Oh, I hope, I hope he did!" Wilkin chortled.

Alvisor cackled in agreement.

The trio began the short but arduous ascent to the flat top of Ikkapoor Mountain.

Chapter 21

The Monster's Last Stand?

"Stop raking me over them coals!" Alvisor shouted. He startled awake and stared at the rake lying across his chest. He had conjured it during his sleep. He shoved the rake aside and stood up.

Roger picked his face up. His disobedient countenance had persisted in lying on the brown sand even after he had been standing limply erect and reasonably manlike. His pals missed this oddity.

Wilkin spat out a cricket. "Never Trust a cricket," he said foolishly. "Not even a glod bearing one." He nodded.

Alvisor began clapping in three fourths time.

Kissing each of his knees in turn as he did so, Roger danced.

Wilkin played the toe of one of his dwarfin boots as though it were a mini-flute.

"A two and a one and a two and a one," Roger grunted, between each kiss.

"A three and a four and a five and a six," the magician said, with a deeply Southern drawl.

Twoodele, twoodele, twoodele, doo, Wilkin piped merrily on his dwarfin shoe. "Them's sweet notes! Sweet and lovely, lilting notes," he said, with a sigh, and a tiny tear in his gleaming eye.

Alvisor leaped around a bit, still clapping.

Wilkin continued playing his boot-flute.

Both men danced closely after Roger, oblivious to the fact he was leading them toward a steep cliff.

Roger heaved up out of the sand in which he had cleverly been buried. "What the hell you dancing with?" he screeched in horror, awe and maybe jealousy.

"Ieeeeeee!" Wilkin wailed. "It's a fearsome Turnpike come to charm us to our deaths! And it's callously taken on our Earthman's flabby form!" He spat fiercely on the enemy, like an oscillating lawn sprinkler.

Roger marveled at the dwarf's enhanced ability to produce saliva.

The ersatz Roger ceased its gleeful dance. It angrily wiped its eyes.

"I, Alvisor, Magician, First Triple A Class, and semi-retired, shall vanquish you with—" He glanced around, saw his opportunity and grabbed it up off the hot sand. "—this nifty rake!" he jabbed the Turnpike Roger in the throat, sending the beast spinning off the cliff.

The Turnpike changed into a small, oily looking, green cloud. It had one huge eye and a tiny mouth. It floated a few inches from the trio. "Turnpikes can't be killed!" it shrieked. "They can only be avoided!"

"Or ignored," Wilkin said, with uncharacteristic brilliance. He wiped saliva off his chin with the heel of his hand and turned his contemptuous back to the Turnpike.

Alvisor and Roger followed suit, although it really was not clever of the Turnpike to transform itself into an orange zoot suit.

"Come back!" Wilkin pleaded. "He'll wreck your lives!"

The sleeves of the Turnpike suit attempted to pull Roger and Alvisor into a pit of tepid soapy water it conjured. They retreated wildly from the woven monster.

"My glod!" Alvisor swore. "The awesome horror of it leaves me corpse cold!"

"It sure plays dirty," Roger agreed. He had sorely desired that groovy suit to proudly wear.

"I'll bet I'm vastly cleaner than you," the Turnpike retorted, through its lapels, "even though I don't use soap or water!" It landed on the sand and transformed into a giant, cinnamon-hued, Twiddley Button. Twiddley, shimmering like pure glod, was printed across its front.

Wilkin was sorely pressed to possess it as a memento of his much feared Uncle Twiddley. But even his fevered mind knew this was an unclean Turnpike trick. He showed his disdainful back to the hypnotic button.

Roger and Alvisor did likewise.

The Turnpike howled like a defeated politician.

"How long must we sweet and innocent victims withstand this poor man's Homer's Hell?" Roger whispered.

"I was taught it only gets four chances to trick Mr. Death into our repulsed bodies before it dissolves from its humiliating failure," Wilkin said. "It's tried—let me see—" He counted by stomping his foot against the coarse sand like a poorly trained horse.

"Four times!" Alvisor shouted. He performed a short, obscene jig of celebration. "It's done been ignored out of all of its tries!"

The trio looked fearfully around, hoping Wilkin's information was correct, and the infamous Turnpike was forever gone. It is touch and go with all text book learning.

It was and it was.

"I thought you said Turnpikes were only legends?" Roger complained.

"I did," Alvisor said. "But *The Monster's* heard of them legends, *too*. He's probably aware we're still alive and made one of them come to life to kill us. Just like he did with all those other magic traps."

"That is correct, chisel lips," The Monster rumbled from behind. He was standing beside a dune. His gloved hands were raised to cast magic death at his pesterers. "I wasted my priceless time joyfully toying with you reeking, walking worms. I should have destroyed you the instant I learned of Aleron's location. I will rectify this mistake now, of course!" He slipped one glove off, then the other, dropping them at his feet.

Alvisor grabbed up the rake and charged, snorting in rage, something like an underweight, dyspeptic bull.

The Monster thrust his hands out, but too late. The head of the rake caught him square on the chest and he flipped backwards off the mountain.

Alvisor skidded to a stop, just short of pitching over the cliff. He peered down the boulder-strewn mountain side. "He's still bouncing!" he said. "Now he's stopped, busted to dust like he was a stone! In his panic, he musta tried to protect hisself, but chose the wrong method! Thank glod!"

"How very suave, polite and considerate of him," Roger said, with a big, silly grin between his dimples.

"Now that he's gone," Wilkin said, with a wide and obscenely happy smile, "the rest of the trip should be a piece of liver cake!"

"Hey, where's Aleron's place?" Roger said.

"We just have to walk," Alvisor said, as he dropped the rake. Nearby, lay The Monster's gloves, with his emblem on their backs. Alvisor picked them up and put them in a pocket of his robe. "A present for Aleron," he explained.

***

The top of the mountain grew wider and wider. The sky lost its blue, becoming white as though overcast, but there were no clouds. The ringing silence was as profound, and as useless as a philosophical truth.

***

Two towering dunes raised up from the flat sand.

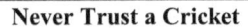

The trio trudged between them in light shadow.

Roger felt like he was inside a sound proof, plastic-covered sand box trying unsuccessfully to reach the end of a tread mill.

***

The dunes grew higher but the light shadow did not darken.

The silence was beginning to get to Wilkin. He was rapping the top of his head with his knuckles, with his mouth open, making weird, arrhythmic noises. Roger and Alvisor raptly listened as though he were a one thousand piece, virtuoso, tuba and drum orchestra performing a haunting, hypnotic sonata.

***

The trio emerged from between the dunes and over a steep rise.

Roger's eyes became affixed on what lay before them. Alvisor and Wilkin noticed his odd expression. They followed his bloodshot, vacuous stare.

"Our deaths are surely near!" Wilkin mourned. He slipped his hands feverishly through his graying hair.

"It's Aleron's Castle!" Alvisor said, with a wail.

Roger gulped as though he were swallowing a bitter, gigantic dose of refined courage.

The towering gloden castle ponderously lowered its wide, silver drawbridge to the albino colored sand.

Chapter 22

Aleron Puts the Pallor On

The drawbridge revealed a small, simple doorway. This was the beginning of a very long, dark, narrow passage.

The awed travelers stood like three odd-sized zombies stiffly awaiting unpleasant instructions.

The command was not long in coming.

A mauve light sprang up and speedily approached.

Roger unreasonably thought of Flaming Jack, a picturesque character he once ran across. He broke into a profuse sweat.

Although he had never seen or heard of one, Wilkin thought of an express train. He began whimpering. He was afraid it was going to eat him and spit out his teeth and ears.

Alvisor reached into his pocket and clutched his glod pouch. He was prepared to flee. To hell with Roger, he thought. I promised to get him here, but I sure didn't say anything about going in with him! His eyes sparkled with happiness. Yeah, he thought. I can leave the ex-fat boy and the nasty little man. I can take my glod to some quiet bar.

Get drunk. Find a woman. And have fun! Cackling to himself, he started to go. He felt Roger's hands slip around his throat and reluctantly turned back to the black opening.

The mauve glow revealed itself to be a black habited figure. It was holding in what resembled a hand a jar filled with what resembled fireflies. Its face was hidden by the hood of the habit. It raised the big jar above its head, ending all chances of the trio seeing its visage. It beckoned in a ghostly fashion, and started down the dark hallway.

The firefly light showed little of the corridor. But Roger was certain he saw cheap burlap on the walls. Like in a horror house trailer at a fair or circus on Earth. He had always hated those.

Wilkin realized he was in the lead. He tried to slink behind his friends.

Roger showed his fists and grinned in a fiendish fashion.

Alvisor prepared to use his beard like a bull whip.

Wilkin faced forward again. He bit his forearm to keep himself from screaming for mercy, forgiveness and the bathroom. Then he concentrated on the guide's back and tried to imagine the figure was really a sexy lady dwarf enticing him to her tiny, plush bedroom.

**

Just as Wilkin was about to improperly fondle the robed figure, the hall ended at a large yellow door.

Their guide rudely ushered them through, slamming

the door and leaving them to their own devices.

The room was illuminated by what resembled ceiling panel lights.

Roger thought the chamber looked like the waiting area in an out-of-date Earth doctor's office.

Uncomfortable wooden chairs lined the light green walls. A red table, covered with dusty magazines, stood in the center of the sky-blue floor. Soft music, which was obviously meant to be soothing, was evident.

The melodies infuriated Roger. He wanted to rip the room apart and stomp on the source until it was nothing but silent debris. "Help me mercy kill this damned music!" he said to Alvisor.

"It won't avail you to try," the Magus said. "That music ain't coming from nowhere but mid air. Why don't you do like Wilkin and look at pretty pictures?"

The dwarf was tearing the pages of a magazine into long, narrow strips and placing them into a neat but vulgar pile on the floor.

Roger shuddered. "No thanks," he said. "I'll just wander around until Aleron comes."

"Whatever you want," Alvisor said. He helped himself to the floor. "Mind if I take a nappo?"

The yellow door at the far side of the room snapped open. A second figure, or for all they knew, the original guide trying to appear to be a different person, beckoned.

Alvisor cursed and got up.

Roger snatched Wilkin to his feet.

They passed down a short, blue-stone hallway illuminated by an undiscoverable source. Suits of shiny armor, spaced by multicolored urns, stood along the walls. One had three legs. Another boasted two helmets.

Roger started to ask Wilkin about this, but decided the little man would not have a likable answer.

They were ushered through a third yellow door into another, but much larger, room lighted by ceiling panels. Rich tapestries blazed red and green on two of the glod walls. An immense Royal-Purple Persian-type rug lay on the floor.

At the far end of the room, crouched a crescent shaped, varnished desk which seemed as huge as the flight deck of an aircraft carrier. A world globe sat on one end, a telescope on the other. Three ebon leather chairs sat in front.

Behind the desk was a high-backed black leather chair and a window Roger estimated as being twenty-five feet high and forty feet wide. Glod-colored velvet drapes were drawn to each side. Only desolate darkness could be seen beyond the glass.

What really caught the weary trio's attention was the man sitting at the desk. He sported a black handle-bar mustache, was midway between Roger and Alvisor in height, and wore a robe identical to Alvisor's but clean, and of a vastly superior cut of cloth.

Roger thought Aleron was a dead ringer for a circus barker.

From somewhere beside the travelers, a circus bark-er voice said: "Come forward, please, and take a chair."

Fighting for last place, they approached the impos-ing desk and seated themselves. Then they got up and headed for separate chairs.

The mighty Wizard of Ikkapoor Mountain grimaced and swiveled his back to his less than desirable guests. When they were finally seated, he swiveled around and flashed the smile of a super slick salesman about to con-vince them to purchase a twenty year subscription to The Stink Weed Grower's Journal. Or some other tawdry, worthless item. "Now, then," he said. "What can I do for you?"

"First," Alvisor quavered, "that dig-happy flower Planter you zapped a while back was brought awake a day or so ago. It chased us a bit, then it fell into the Canyon and busted to pieces. But—"

"Say no more," Aleron said, in an imperial man-ner. One tended to obey him. "Its diggings are as good as filled in. Now, about your problem?"

"I was working a—er—a—spell a couple of days ago," Alvisor said. "Something went unconscionably wrong at the same time lightning flashed outside my Tree and Roger, there's, bedroom.

"He was dreaming The Synchronizing Power Word at the same time and was drawn to my lab from some other god awful planet. He wants to get back to his world because he misses his purposeless existence there. Can you fix him up, and send me and Wilkin, here, back to my comfy old tree house?"

Aleron mused for a suspiciously short moment. "Could be," he said. "Of course, there are lots of things to consider. Glod being foremost." He flashed that super slick Salesman of the Century smile. "I'll tell you what. Since I've never had a case quite like this before, I'll make an exception in yours. I don't do this for everyone, mind you, but—I don't know—I like you, boy and I'm gonna do you a favor. We won't discuss the financial end of our happy arrangement until I produce results. Is that all tight with you?"

Alvisor slapped his hands over his glod bag and sent up a fervent prayer for its protection to Budda. A crafty expression crossed his face, leaving small, wrinkled footprints. "But there's one other thing, sir," he said. "It was *The Monster* who brought the Planter back to life to keep us from warning you he was coming to kill you. You don't have to worry about him, though. I knocked him off a cliff. He turned into stone to protect hisself and busted to dust." He drew the Monster's ebon gloves from his pocket and tossed them across the desk.

Aleron inspected The Monster's insignia. "No kidding," he said. He was unable to hide a smile, and his relief. "In that case, there shall be no charge for my services."

Alvisor's smile was so wide, his ears met on the

back of his head. He patted Roger on the shoulder. "Is it too late to send this fine young fellow back home tonight?" he asked.

"Not at all," Aleron said, heartily. "Any time is the right time for those who do favors for *Aleron*, no matter how insignificant that favor might be. If you'll follow me, please." He pulled one of the velvet drapes aside to reveal a door. This slid open at a touch and he led them into a small, pink cubicle.

Roger recognized it as an elevator.

The door closed and Aleron faced the trio. "Now, young man," he said, "what's your full name?"

"Roger Asbestio Lincoln," Roger admitted.

Alvisor and Wilkin took no notice of Roger's shame. They were more interested in the ugly sinking sensation caused by the elevator.

Aleron sniggered snidely and nodded. "Now," he instructed, "in order to decide upon our best course, tell me about yourself and where you come from."

Roger happily obliged. No one had ever wanted to hear about his life before. Except for a strangely fascinated psychiatrist at the Army Draft Center. And Roger had not been pleased about that.

***

The elevator clicked to a halt.

Wilkin and Alvisor were asleep against one wall.

Aleron had to grab his numb head to stop it from nodding and feigning interest.

The door slid open to a narrow gray-rock corridor illuminated by glowing life sized portraits painted on the walls. At odd intervals, were ominous dark openings.

"Those hallways lead to various ancient dungeons and torture chambers," Aleron cheerily explained. "I've turned them into storerooms," he said. "But, I understand the previous owner, who built this castle, used them constantly. He was a very nasty man-thing. Before I dispatched him to The Cow's Mouth, that is."

"Must have been Mavis's father," Alvisor whispered to Roger.

"See what you missed by not marrying her?" Roger said. "All this spooky shit could have been yours."

"Wouldn't have been worth it considering I'd a had ta face her every gut-wrenching morning!" Alvisor said.

In about ten minutes, the hall of portraits ended at a thick iron door. Aleron preceded them into his laboratory. It was even larger than his ostentatious office, but lighted by big white-glass globes attached at regular intervals to the gray-rock ceiling. A long low stage fashioned from wide boards of black wood filled the far side and was littered with red tables, blue folding screens, and mysterious implements. A dozen wooden chairs were stacked up before it.

The part of the lab in which the trio stood was thick with orange tables covered with flasks, test tubes, Fisher burners, and every other chemist's tool in existence.

The gray-rock walls were lined by black metal shelves filled by cans of ingredients with incredible names like: ClydeKlatch Root Plus Schoo or Preposterous Promp's Reee Greens and Third Arm Removers.

Where there were no shelves or tables there were towering cabinets of gray steel.

Alvisor turned green with envy and hung his head. This place made his lab look like an idiot child's play-room. "If I'd a had a set up like *this*," he told Roger, "you wouldn't of had to go to all this trouble to get home. I'd a returned you there a hour after you zoned down."

"Pull up some chairs and get yourselves comfort-able while I make eerie preparations," Aleron com-manded. He unlocked the nearest cabinet. When he pulled the long doors open, several frilly bras fell at his feet. He ignored them and began thumbing through magic books the size of unabridged dictionaries and God's thumbnail.

The trio unstacked chairs, placed them a short dis-tance from the stage, and sat.

Alvisor opened a bag and started lovingly counting his glod.

Having no magazines to destroy, Wilkin fell asleep.

Roger watched every move Aleron made, expecting instant results.

Aleron placed his aged tomes in their proper order and locked the cabinet. He mounted the stage and dis-appeared behind the largest folding screen.

The light over the center of the stage grew more bright, the others dimmed out.

Wilkin awoke from his deep sleep.

The trio sat up straight and leaned forward in lascivious eagerness. When no strip show began, they slumped back. They were so disappointed, they paid scant attention to Aleron when he entered the pool of white light.

He was pushing a small wheeled table covered with an assortment of bottles, jars, cardboard boxes, beer stains and high-deductible insurance policies.

He produced a piece of white chalk from a pocket of his robe and drew a large pentagram on the stage. He removed five white candles from a box and placed one at each point of the pentagram. He emptied the contents of the various vessels into the exact center of the pentagram, and shoved the table into the darkness. He lit the candles with a very long match, then ignited the pile of ingredients.

A hellish purple fire ensued.

Curiously, the agog trio felt no heat.

After a few moments, the fire transformed into a thick pillar of gray smoke which hung together like a solid. It stood on the stage, almost touching the ceiling.

Roger and company were frightened into the shakes! The Smoke was straining to get at them!

Wilkin jumped down and hid under his chair.

Alvisor held out his precious bag of glod as if offering the Smoke a bribe to leave him in peace, not pieces.

It became obvious the candles were holding the Smoke inside the pentagram.

Roger twisted his eyeballs back into their sockets. He heard Aleron chant some strange, unsettling, guttural words. When he gathered sufficient courage, he peered between his trembling fingers.

The Smoke had turned chartreuse.

Aleron pulled a very long wheel-equipped yellow stepladder out of the dark. He ran up the rungs, produced a clear, plastic-looking crowbar from one of his sleeves and began beating the Smoke. The crowbar rebounded like it was striking rubber.

The Smoke shook twice. It shrank a foot or so and turned blue.

Aleron scrambled down the rungs and vanished into the darkness with the ladder and the crowbar. When he reappeared, he was carrying a foot long, foot round cigarette which he held out at arm's length.

The Smoke projected a tendril, took the fag, and stuck it in an orifice about nine feet above the stage.

Roger could tell it was nine feet because he saw that many purple wooden ones stacked up, heel to toe, nearby.

Aleron reached into his pocket, pulled out a long wooden match, struck it against his nose, and lit the cigarette.

The Smoke subsided to a pastel ocher and puffed

madly on the fag.

Roger peered through the gloom to his left.

Alvisor was raptly watching the stage, oblivious to all else.

Roger peered to his right.

Wilkin was still huddled beneath his chair.

"Is that you, Wilkin?" Roger whispered.

A garbled noise replied.

"What are you doing under there?" Roger said.

"I thought I heard something fall," Wilkin said, hastily, "and decided to see what it was. I figured Alvisor mighta dropped a swak of glod."

"I know you're trying to figure a way to sneak out of here," Roger said, with a grin, "so don't try to fool *me*."

"Hell," Wilkin said. He reluctantly climbed into his chair. "That's what I get for meeting up with a smart-headed belch! Can't conceal my true and actual, cowardly, selfish motives! What do you crave?"

"Aleron's sideshow's got me thinking," Roger said. "And—well. How would you like to live in a place where you felt like the only worm on a planet full of hungry birds?"

Wilkin's eyes glowed red. "My damn! You won't make me go?" he begged, kissing Roger's hand.

Roger slapped him on the forehead. "I'm talking about me!" he snapped. "That's how *I* felt on my world! And without even friends to make it bearable!"

"I can't stand it!" Wilkin said, with a gasp. He waved

his arms, snapping his fingers. "The thought of you being pecked at all of the time! Running! Scared! Hurt-
ing! Bleeding!" He grabbed himself by the throat. "I'd
rather die, now, than see it happen!" He stopped the
execution as inspiration came. His eyes ceased glowing
and he patted Roger on the knee. "You've got friends
here, to comfort and endanger you, so you don't nec-
essarily got to go back, pally," he insinuated.

Roger kissed the dwarf on the forehead. "Yeah," he
chortled. "Yeah! I really don't have to go back! No big
gun's at my nape! No lettuce is in my salad! Nobody's
twisting my teat! I don't have to go back, damn it!"

Aleron started shouting. His back was to his small
audience and he was waving his arms.

The Smoke was running the gamut of colors, looking like an acid rock light show out of control.

Aleron dropped his arms, in disgust, and paced back
and forth, shaking his head. He snapped his fingers and
pulled a large, silver-wheeled blackboard out of the
darkness. He snatched the chalk from his pocket and
drew some figures on the board. He conjured a rod and
pointed out something in the calculations to the Smoke.

The Smoke shifted up and down the color scale and
stopped on blue-green.

Aleron nodded excitedly. He shoved the blackboard
into the darkness, faced the Smoke squarely and issued
it a torrent of commands.

The Smoke turned yellow, stretched upwards and

spat out the fag and several black-iron balls which dented the stage.

Aleron stamped out the cigarette and kicked the orbs out of the way. He jammed a hand into a pocket of his robe, hurled a bit of white powder at the Smoke, and leaped back.

The Smoke shot up and down the color scale, with incredible speed.

Roger saw only a long white blur.

The Smoke stopped on gray. Three feet away, an oblong opening appeared in mid air.

As though a master switch had been thrown, the Smoke vanished, the candles sputtered out and the room lights flowered into their former brilliance.

The Wizard of Ikkapoor Mountain turned to the trio. He beckoned beguilingly to Roger. "Your wish has come true," he said, "the pathway to your world is now open. You may leave whenever you desire."

Roger remained where he was. Now that the time really was at hand, he was not sure: Stay *or* go? Bandits *or* smog? Turnpikes *or* opportunists? Atom bombs *or* friends?

Aleron frowned a little. "But of course," he said, "you naively and insultingly doubt I have been successful. That is only natural." His well oiled facade slipped. "Heave off your laggard, sagging asses, haul up here, and eyeball this breathtaking miracle of interstellar space which I have ingeniously wrought!"

Roger breathlessly stepped onto the low stage. Wilkin and Alvisor meekly followed.

Roger inched to the space warp, peeped in, and sure enough, wonder of wonders, he was seeing the living room of his apartment!

Aleron approached the magic breach and his chin dropped. "Is *that* where you live?" he shouted. "Trade you even!" He leaped through the warp and it whooshed closed almost before Roger could happily blink his eyes.

www.ingramcontent.com/pod-product-compliance
Lightning Source LLC
Chambersburg PA
CBHW070756280626
47162CB00016B/1067